ACCLAIM FOR *SWING* BY OPAL CAREW

"Opal Carew's *Swing* is a blazing hot erotic romp. . . . A must-read for lovers of erotic romance. A fabulously fun and stupendously steamy read for a cold winter's night. This one's so hot, you might need to wear oven mitts while you're reading it!"   —*Romance Junkies*

4 stars! "A beautiful erotic romance . . . real and powerful."
                    —*Romantic Times BOOKreviews*

"*Swing* is fresh, exciting, and extremely sexual, with characters you'll fall in love with. Absolutely fantastic!"   —*Fresh Fiction*

"*Swing* is so much fun to read. . . . The story line is fast-paced, with wonderful humor."   —*Genre Go Round Reviews*

ACCLAIM FOR *TWIN FANTASIES* BY OPAL CAREW

4 stars! "Carew's devilish twists and turns keep the emotional pitch of the story moving from sad to suspenseful to sizzling to downright surprising in the end. . . . The plot moves swiftly and satisfyingly."   —*Romantic Times BOOKreviews*

"Opal Carew brings erotic romance to a whole new level . . . she writes a compelling romance and sets your senses on fire with her love scenes!"   —*Reader to Reader*

4 stars! "Written with great style . . . *Twin Fantasies* is surely a must for any erotic romance fan, ménage enthusiasts in particular."
                    —*Just Erotic Romance Reviews*

"*Twin Fantasies* is plain delicious in its sensuality. Opal Carew has a great imagination and her sensual scenes are sure to get a fire going in many readers."   —*A Romance Review*

ALSO BY OPAL CAREW

Swing
Twin Fantasies

blush

Opal Carew

ST. MARTIN'S GRIFFIN

NEW YORK

To Matthew,

who inspires me
with his intelligence,
compassion,
and desire to make
the world a better place.

You make my world a better place
just by being in it!

BLUSH. Copyright © 2008 by Elizabeth Batten-Carew. All rights reserved. Printed in the United States of America. For information, address St. Martin's Press, 175 Fifth Avenue, New York, N.Y. 10010.

www.stmartins.com

Library of Congress Cataloging-in-Publication Data

Carew, Opal.
    Blush / Opal Carew.—1st ed.
        p.   cm.
    ISBN-13: 978-0-312-36779-4
    ISBN-10: 0-312-36779-1
    1. Sex (Psychology)—Fiction.   I. Title.

PR9199.4.C367 B58 2008
813'.6—dc22   2008012430

10 9 8 7 6 5 4 3

one

"I want an orgasm." Hanna Lane's hands clenched in her lap as she stared at her sister across the table.

Grace cleared her throat.

"I think the drink is called a Screaming Orgasm," Grace said, loud enough for the people around them to hear.

They both knew that wasn't what Hanna had meant. Hanna glanced around the restaurant and noticed people staring at them, and her cheeks flushed hotly. She lowered her voice. "I'm sorry, I'm just a tad frustrated."

"I'll bet. Have you tried one of those vibrators with the thing—"

"Yes, it doesn't work. Nothing works," Hanna answered shortly, not wanting to talk sex toys with her older sister. Hanna didn't want to have this conversation at all, but she didn't know who else to turn to.

Grace patted Hanna's hand. "You'll find someone soon. When you're in a relationship again—"

"No, it won't matter."

"Honey, I know what you and Grey had was very special, but you'll find someone special again, and with him—"

"No, you don't understand. Grey and I never . . ." She stared into Grace's intense gaze. "I mean, I've never . . ."

"Ever?"

Hanna shook her head, her gaze fixed on the water glass in front of her and the condensation beading on the crystal surface.

"Even with Grey? But he was so sexy. And considerate, and patient."

Hanna nodded. "I know. It wasn't his fault."

Grace nodded. "That's true. The only person who can give you an orgasm is you. You have to let it happen."

"You're not going to tell me just to relax, are you? If I hear that one more time, I'm going to scream."

She'd read every book she could find on the subject, and they all insisted that the woman just had to relax and allow it to come. But it wasn't that simple.

Grace's lips pursed as she watched Hanna.

"Why haven't you told me about this before?"

"It isn't exactly the kind of thing you want to go running to your big sister about."

Grace squeezed Hanna's hand. "It is *exactly* the kind of thing you can come running to me about, honey." She paused. "Is that why you broke up with Grey?"

Hanna had known her sister would ask that. After all, Hanna and Grey had seemed perfect for each other. In fact, they *were* perfect for each other, except for one thing. In the year they'd been together, he had never once told her he loved her.

Which had hurt all the more because she loved him so much.

There was a time she'd dreamed of happily-ever-after in Grey's arms. She'd even convinced herself that he was just one of those guys who found it hard to say the words.

But she needed to hear them. She had to know he actually loved her.

Finally, she'd thought if she said the words first, he would reciprocate. One day, in their favorite restaurant, she had taken his hand in hers and gazed into his warm green eyes glimmering in the candlelight.

"Grey, I love you," she'd said.

His fingers stiffened within her grip and his smile faded.

"Grey," she'd prompted him. "Did you hear me?"

"Yes, of course. I just have to . . ." He'd glanced around, as if seeking an escape, then stood up. "I have to call the office."

He'd rushed away from the table like a man pursued by a demon, then returned a few minutes later and continued with dinner as if their previous conversation had never happened.

She'd gotten the message loud and clear.

A week later, after a lot of soul-searching, she had broken up with him. She'd told him that she loved him, but he clearly didn't love her. A part of her, even at that point, had hoped he'd deny it, then sweep her into his arms and proclaim his love for her. Instead, he'd only looked shocked.

Then she'd asked him outright, "Do you love me?"

He'd drawn in a deep breath and taken her hand in his. "The way I feel about you is different from what I've felt for any other woman. Deeper. I love having you in my life."

"But do you *love* me?"

His mouth had tightened into a flat line and he'd said no more.

She'd simply nodded at that point, knowing she had lost.

Pain lanced through her at the memory. She still loved him and she missed him every single day . . . and night. She'd always felt loved and cherished, snuggled in his arms in bed.

Tears welled in her eyes and she dashed them away.

"Oh, honey." Grace pulled her into a warm embrace and patted her back.

Hanna accepted her big sister's hug, then slowly drew away, still thinking about Grey. "We just weren't right for each other."

How could she settle for less than love? How could she ask Grey to settle for less?

Grace looked skeptical, but she let the subject drop.

"Okay, honey, what are you doing to solve the problem?"

Hanna's sister, who was a holistic healer, was a firm believer that everyone was responsible for their own problems . . . and solutions.

"I've been reading books." Hanna gazed at Grace. "And I'm talking to you."

Grace's eyes glowed with warmth and she smiled.

"There's a ten-week course at the university, in the evenings. I believe it starts next week. I know the guy who's teaching it, and he's exceptional."

Hanna's eyes narrowed. "What kind of course?"

"It's called 'Kama Sutra for the Beginner,' but he discusses different sexual issues, and one of the things he talks about is female orgasm and the fact that a lot of women have trouble achieving it. I know the instructor and I've recommended a couple of my patients take the workshop."

"I'm already signed up."

"You are?" Grace's eyebrows rose. Obviously, she didn't believe her.

Grey had signed them up for that course, hoping it would help her with her problem. Now that they'd broken up, though, she couldn't bear to take the course alone. Not that she would tell Grace that.

Taking the course would remind Hanna of the frustration she and Grey had both shared. It would remind her how hard he had tried to make sex enjoyable for her, despite her problem.

It would remind her that she no longer had Grey in her life.

"You know . . ." Grace stared at Hanna over the frosty water glass she held in her hand. "The instructor's single. . . ."

"Forget it."

Grace sipped her water, then placed her glass on the table.

"Okay, so why don't you do something wild and different? Something you've never done before?"

"Like what?"

"Well, maybe find some sexy guy—someone you don't even know—and make wild, passionate love with him. If you don't know him, you can act differently. You don't have to be yourself. You can be wild and uninhibited. Maybe then you can let go of what's holding you back."

Wild and uninhibited. Hanna's stomach tightened.

"Oh, no, I don't think so."

"Why not?"

"A complete stranger? That's crazy."

"Sometimes you need to let loose. Do something crazy. But it doesn't have to be a complete stranger. It could be someone you've seen a few times. Maybe been attracted to. You could even form a relationship after . . . or not. The point is not to worry about it. That's where the freedom lies."

Goose bumps shivered down her spine. The thought actually excited her. How insane was that?

In fact, she thought about the tall, sexy man who'd started coming to the Hot Spot Café, the coffee shop she owned, about a month ago. He had eyes the color of espresso and a deep, melodic voice that sent tingles down her spine every time he spoke. And he was exceptionally good-looking, with a strong, straight nose and a square jaw softened by the waves of dark curls that caressed his collar.

She had found herself making an excuse to help out behind the counter whenever he came in so that she could serve him. Organic Earl Grey tea with milk and natural cane sugar. He was always warm and friendly, and he exuded a sexual magnetism that sent her senses whirling and had triggered some exciting and embarrassingly erotic dreams.

Maybe her sister's suggestion wasn't so crazy after all.

J.M. walked along the stone path through the campus, lit by the streetlights and the soft glow of an almost full moon. A light, warm breeze rustled through the trees as he stepped toward the traffic light on the corner of Stevens Street and Main, Brock University campus behind him.

He liked it here in Spring Falls, a quaint university town where the people were friendly, the pace was easy, and the scenery was stunning. The Shannonista River meandered through town, banked by bike paths and parks filled with flowering shrubs and bright gardens.

Ordinarily, he would head straight home at this hour, but he had a craving for an Earl Grey tea, the special blend with bergamot oil they served in the coffee shop across from the campus. Or, really, a craving to see the attractive woman who frequently served him.

He smiled at the thought of her midnight blue eyes twinkling as her soft, rose lips curled up in a smile, which happened every time she turned and saw him at the front of her line. She wore her long, blond hair tied back, but soft wisps swirled around her heart-shaped face and caressed her cheeks. There was a sweet innocence about her, but he sensed a smoldering sexuality beneath the surface.

The light turned and he crossed the street. It was unlikely she'd be on duty now, since he usually saw her there in the late afternoon, but it didn't really matter. All they'd ever done was exchange a few friendly words while he'd waited for his tea. Of course, if the shop was still open, which he doubted on a Thursday night at nine thirty . . . and if she was there . . . and if the opportunity presented itself . . . then maybe he'd ask her out.

His intuition told him this could be his lucky night.

The bell over the door rang and Hanna hurried to finish clearing the tray of dishes, wishing she'd locked the door after the last customer had left a few moments ago.

"I'll be with you in a moment," she said over her

shoulder as she wiped the tray and placed it on the stack of clean ones.

She was still here forty minutes after closing. There had been a rush of people about a quarter to nine, and they'd just kept coming in. Someone had mentioned there'd been a special speaker at the psychology building tonight and the talk had ended at eight thirty.

She turned around and stopped cold as she found herself facing the tall, dark-haired man she'd been dreaming about even before her sister suggested she jump a stranger. Her cheeks flushed and a tremor of awareness quivered through her body.

"I'm sorry, I didn't mean to startle you." He smiled. "I'm glad you're still open."

"Well, actually, we aren't." Oh, damn, why had she said that? "I mean, I can still get you something, but . . . I'm just closing up now."

"You're sure?"

"Of course. I haven't turned off the machine yet, and there's still plenty of hot water." She smiled but glanced toward the door, hoping no one else would come in. "An Earl Grey? I have decaf if you'd like. Naturally decaffeinated."

"That would be great."

Her gaze strayed to the large front window and a couple walking by, gazing into the shop. Hanna grabbed the key from the drawer under the till.

"Look, would you mind locking the door for me?" She placed the key with the brass cup-and-saucer key chain on the counter. "It's actually past closing time and I don't want any more customers tonight."

"Absolutely."

She grabbed a tall mug from the shelf and filled it with hot water, then ripped open the foil pouch on the tea bag as he walked across the store. When she heard the click of the lock, she realized she was in the shop all alone at night with a sexy, attractive man. One she'd been having hot dreams about. Dreams where they'd done intimate, erotic things together.

She dipped the bag in the steaming water until it reached the darkness she knew he liked and filled the mug with milk and one packet of cane sugar, then placed it on the maple counter. He placed the key beside it, along with a couple of bills to pay for the tea.

"I was going to take it to go so I wouldn't keep you."

She stared at the ceramic mug she'd given him.

"Oh, sorry. I can put it in a takeout cup . . . or . . . you're welcome to enjoy it here, if you like. I've . . . uh . . . got some leftover banana walnut muffins I can't serve tomorrow." Great, she'd just offered him what sounded like stale muffins. "On the house."

She lifted the glass cover from the decorative plate containing three muffins, picked up the tongs, and placed the biggest, fattest muffin on a plate and handed it to him.

He smiled. "Thank you. These are my favorite."

She knew that. He ordered them every time they had

some, so she'd added them to the menu more often, just in case he came by.

She dropped the rest in a paper bag and curled the top.

"Actually, take the rest, too. I'd just wind up taking them home, and I don't need any more muffins."

As he took the bag, his hand brushed hers and an explosion of sensation burst along her arm. She had to work at not snatching her hand away.

"Are you this generous with all your customers?"

"No, not really. I . . . uh . . ." She paused, worried he would think she was flirting with him, then realized that's exactly what she was doing. She just wasn't very good at it. "I just hate to see them go to waste."

She *really* wasn't good at this!

"Here's to finding myself locked in a coffee shop with a cup of tea, a muffin . . . and a beautiful woman." He held up his mug. "Would you join me?"

His warm, inviting smile chased away any thoughts of refusal.

She smiled shyly. "Okay."

Someone tried the doorknob, rattling the door a little. When the man peered in, she shook her head, mouthing, *We're closed.*

"I . . . uh . . . need to turn down the lights so people know we're closed, otherwise that'll keep happening."

She dimmed the lights, then grabbed a bottle of water

from the cooler and followed him to the table with the two love seats in the far corner. It was in the back of the seating area and people couldn't see them from the window.

"This is nice," she said as she sat across from him.

She watched him as he sipped his tea, her gaze straying to his lips. Full and sexy. She could imagine them pressed against the back of her hand, playing along her knuckles. Goose bumps blossomed along her arm as she thought of those lips taking a long, leisurely stroll up her arm, then nuzzling her collarbone. He would stroke behind her ear, then tip her chin up and capture her lips in a firm, passionate kiss.

Oh, man, she wanted him. Maybe her sister was right. Maybe Hanna should just jump him here and now. Have a sexual romp totally devoid of relationship or baggage. Just consume each other's bodies in a hot, wicked flight of fancy.

But how could she be so bold? Her gaze shifted from his lips to his hot, simmering eyes and her breasts swelled with the need to feel his hands on them. His lips. She wanted him. Here. Now.

"Exactly what are you thinking?" he asked.

"I was thinking that . . ."

She drew in a deep breath, seeking the courage to say what she wanted to say.

J.M. watched her as she licked her lips. This sweet, innocent nymph clearly had passion on her mind. He could feel the desire radiating from her. But he could see she was struggling with how to act on her desire. The hot look of lust in her eyes sent his blood boiling and his cock straining.

She needed a little help getting over her inhibitions —clearly she'd never done this before—and he was determined to help her get what she wanted. Because it was exactly what he wanted, too.

He leaned over the table toward her.

"I'll tell you what I'm thinking."

His gaze shifted to her lips and lingered, just as hers had on his.

"Yes?" She seemed mesmerized.

"I'm thinking how lovely it would be to kiss your luscious lips. To feel their softness against mine."

Her eyes glittered in the dim light.

"Me, too."

two

Hanna pushed herself to her feet and slid beside him on the love seat. All kinds of bells rang in her head, trying to prevent her from continuing, but the heat inside her, swelling inside her breasts and melting through her core, wouldn't let her.

She sat beside him, staring into his eyes. Her nostrils filled with his spicy, masculine scent. She breathed deeply, filling her lungs with his male aroma. Filling her with need.

He made no move toward her. He just watched her, his dark eyes encouraging. Courage built within her and she raised her hand to touch his cheek. Raspy. Oh, so masculine. She stroked his other cheek, loving the maleness of stubby whiskers under her fingertips.

He was so sexy . . . so incredibly attractive. Yet so comfortable to be with. Most sexy men seemed arrogant, making her self-conscious. Grey, too, had been easy to be around right from the beginning. But she didn't want to think about Grey right now.

At this instant, she wanted to lose herself in this man's simmering espresso-colored eyes. She could melt from the heat of his gaze. He made her feel attractive and desirable. Sexy and feminine.

Slowly, she eased forward, approaching those full, masculine lips, anticipating the feel of them on hers. He eased forward just a little. Offering his mouth. Encouraging her.

Simply sitting still used a great deal of J.M.'s considerable discipline. He had to still the lustful desire to pull her into his arms and devour her lips. Loving a woman should be long and slow, but with her he wanted it now. Fast and furious. His cock stirred at the thought, pushing against its black denim prison.

But J.M. took a deep breath and calmed his mind and his body. He would wait for her.

Her lips settled on his, lightly, like the touch of a butterfly's wing. He let out a shuddering breath at the delicate feel of her. She smelled like roses and jasmine, with a tantalizing trace of vanilla.

Why this delightful woman, who his intuition told him had never done anything like this before, had decided to pursue a sensual experience with him, a virtual stranger, he didn't know. He also sensed she was seeking more than an illicit sexual romp.

Her lips began to move on his—slowly, seductively—as she stroked her fingers along his cheeks, then over his temples. She made a tiny strangled sound in her throat, then her fingers tangled in his hair, and she pulled his face tighter to hers, her tongue pulsing against his lips, then slipping inside his mouth. He greeted her with a gentle stroke of his tongue, while hers darted inside and undulated against him.

His pulse increased and he felt his base chakra energy rise to his sacral chakra, sending heat cycling between them, charging him with sweet, sexual energy. He hadn't even touched her body yet and his cock, in full, hard erection, ached for her.

She drew back, their lips parting, and she stared at him with wide, innocent eyes.

"I've never done anything like this before. I—"

He touched a fingertip to her lips. "I know."

He cupped her cheeks within his palms and tilted her chin up as he stared into her midnight blue eyes. His lips captured hers in a sweet, lingering kiss.

"You are a very special, sexy woman and I am honored you have chosen me to explore this side of your sexuality. It is exciting and sensual." He kissed her palm. "Thank you."

Hanna stared at him in astonishment. *How sexy is that?*

She flicked open her top button, then the next. His gaze followed her fingers down the button placket with great interest. When she reached her skirt waistband, she tugged her blouse free, then continued. After she unfastened the last button, she hesitated.

She didn't know this man. How could she do this?

His searing gaze met hers, and beyond the clear sexual desire she saw in those eyes she felt warmth. An appreciation for her as a woman and as a person. She could tell this was a very compassionate man with a loving attitude toward others. Maybe she just saw what she wanted to see, but that was enough for now.

She drew open her white silk blouse, revealing her lace-clad breasts. His gaze grew hotter and more intense. Thank heaven she'd worn her favorite sexy black lace bra and thong today.

She grasped his hand and drew it to her breast, anxious for his touch. The feel of his big, masculine hand cupping her soft flesh sent a thrill rushing through her. Her nipples hardened and her sex clenched in anticipation, desire melting through her.

She dropped her blouse over her shoulders, letting it slip to the floor. In a moment, he would see her naked breasts. A tremor quivered through her as she reached around behind her to unfasten her bra, but he stilled her movements.

"Let me."

She nodded. He caressed her ribs as his hands slid around her, then worked at the hooks. The garment loosened and he drew the cups forward, freeing her breasts.

As the cool air washed across them, the nipples tightened even more.

He smiled as his tender gaze caressed her nipples, tormenting them with sweet pleasure. She longed for his physical touch—almost moaned with the need. He leaned forward and stroked his cheek against one nipple, the burn of raspy whiskers sending hot need blazing through her. He caressed the other with a light brush of his fingertips and she moaned as she clutched his head against her chest. He turned his head and captured one nipple in his hot, wet mouth.

"Oh, yes," she whispered.

She couldn't believe she sat here, in the dim light of her coffee shop, her breast being suckled by a complete stranger. And one so sweet and tender as this. She didn't even know his name, yet his tongue swirled over her nipple and a need burned deep inside her to feel his body pressed tight against her while his cock slid into her, then thrust over and over again.

Her hand slid down his shirt. She could feel his tight, muscular chest, then the solid ridges of his firm abdomen. Her fingers found his belt buckle and, as she fumbled with it, he took her other nipple in his mouth and sucked. At the thrilling sensations spiking through her, her fingers fell slack, so he unlatched his belt and drew the zipper down, leaving him open to her seeking hands. At the thought of his hot, hard shaft waiting for her, she slid her fingers inside his pants and stroked over the soft cotton of his briefs, feeling the solid length of his cock.

She wanted it inside her. She wanted to ride it hard, to feel it invading her deepest, most private places.

She stood up, her gaze locking on his, and unzipped her skirt, then dropped it to the floor. She hooked her fingers in the elastic waist of her black lace thong and rolled it down her legs, then kicked it aside. Now, she stood totally naked in front of him, except for her black patent high heels. He smiled and stood up. He kicked off his shoes, then dropped his pants and unfastened his shirt buttons. She watched in excitement as his shirt slid away, revealing more of his tanned, masculine flesh. Tight, well-sculpted muscles defined his chest and abs. His charcoal briefs barely contained his growing erection. He tugged those down, too, and tossed them aside, revealing a long, thick cock pointing toward her like a divining rod.

He skimmed his hands down her sides, then wrapped them around her waist and drew her forward. Her breasts tingled as they came into contact with his hard, masculine chest, the coarse, curly hair brushing across her sensitive nipples, arousing them more.

He hugged her close, capturing her lips, taking them with a passion matching her own. She melted against him, loving the feel of his body pressed against the length of hers, his hard cock tight against her belly.

"I can't believe how sexy you are," he murmured against her ear. "I'm a very lucky man."

His words calmed and excited her at the same time.

Her hands stroked over his tight, hard butt, her fingertips pressing into his flesh. She drew her hands over his
hips, then eased him backward, onto one of the armless
wooden chairs next to the love seat. She knelt in front of
him and admired his long, steel-hard cock standing
straight up in front of her. She wrapped one hand around
it and stroked. It was amazingly tall and thick. The bulbous head called to her and she leaned forward and licked
it. His eyes drifted closed as she drew it into her mouth
and licked around the crown.

It was glorious feeling his big, thick cock head in her
mouth. She sucked and licked like it was a delicious lollipop, then dove downward, taking him as deep as she
could. She slid up and down several times, to his groans of
appreciation, then slipped off and licked his shaft, from
base to tip.

His hands cupped her face and he drew her forward,
then kissed her lips. He stood up, drawing her to her feet,
and eased her backward. She felt the love seat behind her
calves and sat down. When he knelt in front of her and
parted her legs, she felt a bit panicky. She didn't think she
could allow him to do *that*. Not this stranger.

As he lowered his head, his gaze intent on her glistening slit, she tucked her hands under his chin and lifted.

"No. I'm not comfortable with . . ." Her words trailed
off.

What could she say? She knew it was strange that she
was ready to make love with him—wanted to feel his

cock drive deep into her—but she wouldn't allow him this. It was just too intimate.

But he nodded and smiled.

"Whatever you want."

She nodded, then held out her hand. He grasped it, then stood up and eased her to her feet. She kissed him, then guided him to the chair again. He sat down and she straddled his thighs, then leaned toward him. He captured first one needy nipple, then the other in his mouth and suckled until they throbbed. She wrapped her hand around his cock and pointed it toward her vagina. She eased downward a little and stroked her wet slit with his cock head.

Oh, God, it felt incredible. She dripped with need. Slowly, she sank down. His steel-hard cock stretched her as he ascended into her heated body, stroking her inner walls.

She sat facing him, eye to eye, his immense cock embedded inside her.

"Wow."

Her breathy word made J.M.'s head spin.

Her hot, wet body surrounded him and, even with his years of Tantric training, giving him the ability to hold off ejaculation over hours and hours of lovemaking, he felt he might erupt inside her at any moment. She was that sexy.

He wrapped his arms around her and drew her against him, their chakras aligned. He pulled in a deep breath. As the air washed through his body he imagined beautiful golden light washing through his chakras, calming his body, yet filling him with wonderful energy.

Sitting still, his cock jutting into her, he nuzzled the side of her neck. She sighed, then stroked his shoulders. The delicate sensation of her touch danced across his senses, filling him with a sense of wonder. Her energy, so light, so joyous, filled him with bliss. He kissed across her jawbone, then nibbled her lower lip. Her tongue stroked his lips, then dove inside his mouth, and he sucked it gently, then kissed her earnestly, his tongue dancing with hers as their lips pulsed against each other.

She began to move, pivoting her hips to drive him deeper. Back and forth. A sensual rhythm that stroked his cock, building heat between them.

Hanna felt light-headed as his long, hard cock stroked her sex. What an incredible feeling. And his lips—first nuzzling her neck and lighting a fire within her, now caressing hers with a blazing passion.

Pleasure pulsed within her, building higher and higher. The gentle pressure of his hands, first on her shoulders, then gliding down her sides and over her hips, heated her body even more, sending goose bumps dancing across her flesh.

He tightened his hands on her hips, stilling her movements. His lips parted from hers, then he traveled down her body, kissing and licking his way to her breasts. When he drew one nipple into his hot mouth, she gasped. His cock twitched inside her, and her intimate muscles contracted around it. It felt like a hot, hard marble shaft within her.

She squeezed and released, squeezed and released, gripping his cock, cheered on by its fervent twitching. She felt the upsurge of sexual energy within her again, a mounting pleasure coiling through her cells.

He stroked her other breast and his fingers slid to her hard nipple, then toyed with it, sending an aching need spiraling through her.

She began to move again, rocking on his cock. It thrust within her, stroking her deep inside. So hard. So full. Pleasure built higher. Her muscles tightened. She clutched his shoulders.

So sweet, so good. His cock stroked her insides. She squeezed him again. Waves of blissful sensations washed through her. She sucked in a deep breath as she realized the prize drew nearer. Just beyond reach. She could almost touch it.

Oh, God, she wanted this orgasm.

The pleasure built to a pounding crescendo. Closer. And closer. Her muscles tightened, her whole body taut as a fully wound spring.

So close. His cock—hard and masculine—pounding into her.

The pleasure building.

She wanted it so bad.

Maybe this would work. Maybe this sexy stranger would give her what she needed. That all-elusive orgasm.

Oh, God, she hoped so.

He stroked her back, then grasped her hips, trying to still her movements again, but she pulled free, pounding down on him, racing toward her goal. Tightening her muscles around him as though she could milk it from him.

The pleasure climbed . . . climbed . . .

Then slowed . . . hovering so close but . . . She wailed in frustration. Not close enough.

"Oh, please," she gasped on a long breath. "I'm so close. Make me come." She clutched his shoulders tightly as she rode him mercilessly, grinding his pelvis beneath her own. "Please!" she wailed to the universe in general.

He cupped her behind and kneaded as she continued to ride him. His caresses sent warmth through her, nudging the pleasure up, starting the race again . . .

But it was only a sprint and she started to lose it again. She could feel the orgasm slipping from her grasp, disappearing into a black hole in the distance.

Gone.

Exhausted, her muscles taut and aching, she slowed.

His cock remained long and hard within her. He hadn't come yet.

She kissed his cheek and pushed her stressed muscles further as she began to move again, determined to take him to his climax.

"Sweetheart. It's okay. You don't have to keep going."

She kissed him soundly on the lips. "I want you to come."

As J.M. stared into her eyes, he realized she didn't just want him to . . . she needed him to. Ordinarily, he would hold off his orgasm until she came, but it was clear that she wasn't going to. She was coiled far too tightly. He had tried to slow her down, tried to get her to relax so he could help her build her pleasure slowly, but she had resisted.

He had a great deal of experience helping women who had trouble coming to orgasm—enough to know she would not orgasm tonight. She was too tense and too frustrated. If he could take her somewhere quiet and comfortable and spend time relaxing her and building her pleasure over time, he could probably get her there, but that's not what this encounter was about.

She had wanted a forbidden joining of strangers and he didn't think she'd take well to him inviting her home.

So even though she hadn't come, she needed *him* to come. It was a matter of self-esteem, written clearly in her wide midnight blue eyes. He cupped her round ass and stood up, lifting her with him. He leaned her against the wall and thrust forward. This would fit her sex-with-a-stranger fantasy. Hard and fast against a wall. He took care to keep them in the shadows, blocked from the main window by a pillar.

He thrust again and again, releasing his sexual energy to flow free and easy.

"You are so incredibly sexy," he murmured against her ear.

She gasped as he plunged deep inside her and her legs tightened around him in a death grip. She didn't seem to realize that her tension only pushed her orgasm further away. Or maybe she did but was helpless to stop it.

He continued thrusting, luxuriating in the astounding pleasure of his cock gliding along the walls of her vagina. So hot. So wet. So tremendously sensual.

His balls tightened and he pushed aside the automatic reaction to hold off his ejaculation. Her soft breasts pulsed against his chest as he drove into her in short, deep thrusts. The energy built, filling his chakras with intense, cosmic energy, flooding his body with bliss. The sexual energy he had built up over the past few weeks overflowed and his cock swelled, then erupted within her. His body shuddered in orgasm, accompanied by his long, rumbling groan.

He held her close and tight within his arms, his muscles aching from supporting her weight, but not wanting to let her go. Finally, she shifted, then eased her legs down so her feet touched the floor.

"Hanna, you are an incredible woman. Thank you." He kissed her, enjoying her warm, naked body pressed against him, his cock still embedded in the warmth of her body.

Hanna stared into his dark eyes, embarrassment rising within her. She could feel the heat of a blush stain her cheeks.

"How do you know my name?" She had not introduced herself.

He smiled. "You usually wear a name badge."

Oh, damn. So much for anonymity.

What had she done?

Hanna cradled her knees against her chest as she stared at the streetlights visible through the sheer curtains covering the large picture window in her living room. Her big, comfy chair wrapped around her as she rocked her body slightly, remembering the handsome stranger who had risen to her challenge, so to speak.

He had risen quite nicely, in fact. Her cheeks burned at the thought.

She sucked in a breath. How could she have been so wanton? She didn't even know his name.

Which made the whole situation even hotter.

She had to admit, it had been extremely sexy stripping off her clothes in front of him, watching his eyes darken with lust. Then he'd pulled off his shirt, revealing his taut, muscle-ridged abdomen. Her fingers tensed at the memory, wanting to stroke over his hot, masculine flesh once again.

Her stomach churned. Sex with a total stranger. She couldn't believe she'd actually done such a thing. What would people think if they knew?

The memory still haunted her. The feel of his long, hard cock sliding inside her still made her hot. A stolen moment in time. A hot, hard stranger thrusting into her.

The phone rang and she snatched it from its cradle.

"Hello?" Her voice came out hoarse, so she cleared her throat.

"Hanna? You okay?" It was Grey's voice.

three

Hanna's stomach clenched and guilt seeped through her. She felt like she'd been caught doing something wrong. Which was ridiculous. She hadn't cheated on Grey. She had broken up with Grey over two months ago.

She breathed deeply, calming her roiling emotions.

"Grey. Hi. I'm fine. How's New York?"

He'd been offered the chance to do a six-month contract in New York just before they broke up. Actually, the timing had helped her decide to go ahead with the breakup when she did. He wouldn't have gone if they were still together, but it gave him a great chance to spend some time with his mother and two of his sisters who still lived there.

Her heart aching, she picked up the small brass clock that had belonged to Grey's father, which sat on the end table, and stroked her finger along the smooth, round edge. She'd let Grey leave his stuff at her place until he got back and found a place of his own to get settled into.

Unfortunately, having his stuff around constantly reminded her of him.

Reluctantly, she put the clock down. Maybe she should
have insisted he move the stuff into storage, but she'd hated
to say no.

"Mom's happy to have me here, and I had dinner
with Sylvia and her husband last Sunday," he said.

Hanna's heart stung at the sound of his strong, familiar voice, reminding her how much she missed him. How
much she loved him.

"That's great."

"Yeah."

She could just hear the implied, *But I'd rather be there
with you.*

Of course, Grey would never say something like that.
He wasn't the type to share his feelings.

But she could tell by his tone that he wasn't happy
about their breakup, and she hoped he wasn't calling to
try to change her mind. "Are you still going to take the
Kama Sutra course next week?" he asked.

She glanced at the catalog of adult courses from the
university sitting on her coffee table. She'd been reading
the synopsis earlier this evening, trying to decide.

"I don't know."

"You should really think about it. It would be good
for you."

She gripped the phone tighter.

"I don't think I'd want to do it alone."

"Would it help or hurt to tell you I'm still willing to go?"

She didn't even consider telling him it didn't make sense for him to drive the two hours from New York every Tuesday night, because she knew if he got it into his head it was a good idea, he wouldn't listen.

The silence strung tightly between them as she struggled with what to tell him. She could just see the tightening of his jaw as he held back the urge to try to convince her.

"I'll arrange to get the refund and send it to you," she said.

"I don't care about that. I just care about you."

Her chest tightened at his words. It was the closest he'd ever come to saying the *L* word.

J.M. walked into the Astra Alternative Health Care Center on South Garner Street about two blocks from the university and smiled at the friendly redheaded receptionist.

"Hi, Tanya."

She returned his smile.

"Hello, Jeremy." She handed him a clipboard with the latest sheet from his patient information log clipped to the top.

He jotted down what he wanted to work on this visit, which was removing any blocks to his book coming together. He wanted it to be a great success, of course, and to help many people. He believed in putting the right attitude and energy into a project right from the beginning. It helped keep him focused. He initialed the sheet and handed it back to Tanya.

"Great. Dr. Grace will be with you in a moment."

Dr. Grace Jones was the owner of the center and had been his health-care practitioner since he'd moved to Spring Falls a couple of months ago.

As he sat down in one of the upholstered waiting room chairs and gazed out over the tree-filled park beside the center, a gray squirrel pranced across the grass, his cheeks packed full of nuts. J.M. couldn't stop thinking about his enchanting encounter with the beautiful Hanna. She'd been so sensual and sexy yet had somehow maintained an air of shyness and innocence.

His sacral chakra blossomed with energy just thinking about her.

"Hey, Jeremy. How's the book going?"

He glanced around to see Dr. Grace walking his way. He and Grace had become friends over his brief time in town. She was funny and smart and very insightful, sharing many of his same interests, especially in the realm of energy healing.

"I'm still researching and trying to figure out how to put it together. I should be starting it next week."

"And you start your workshop at the university tonight, right?" She picked up his clipboard and led him to her office. She closed the door behind him and he sat down on one of the two chairs facing each other.

"That's right."

She sat down in the other chair. "It turns out my sister is taking your course."

He smiled. "Thanks for recommending me."

"Oh, no, I didn't." She grinned. "I mean, not that I don't recommend you, but my sister . . . well, she's younger than me, so she won't listen to anything I say. Thinks I try to run her life."

"Which, of course, you do."

She rolled her eyes. "Yeah, well. Sometimes it needs a little managing. Anyway, she's got a very specific problem. She's having trouble having an orgasm and—"

"Grace, maybe you shouldn't be telling me this."

"Why not? You're an expert on the subject. I just thought maybe you could give her a little extra help."

He arched his eyebrows upward.

"And what do you want me to do? Take her aside and tell her you told me about her little problem and asked me to help her out?"

She chuckled. "Yeah, right. I'd never hear the end of it if she knew I'd told you. No, I thought you could just stress that topic a little, maybe give specific suggestions. To the class as a whole, you know?"

"Sure, I could do that. A lot of women have that problem."

"Of course, I bet she'd benefit a lot from some personal attention. . . ."

The glint in Grace's eyes told him what kind of personal attention she was hinting at.

"Grace, if you're asking me to date her—"

She grinned wickedly. "We could consider it professional services. You let me know how much time you spend with her, then I'll give you a credit toward your appointments here as payment."

He chuckled at her dry humor. "And how would it look, me dating one of my students?"

She waved a dismissive hand. "No problem. I could easily steer her clear of your course. All I'd have to do is push her to take it. That would send her running."

Grace loved to kid around, but he was beginning to think she actually hoped he would wind up dating her sister. Not that Grace would actually pay him, or anything of the sort, but she had succeeded in setting him up to pay attention to this sister of hers, and since he and Grace got along so well, he had a strong feeling he might be attracted to her sister.

Under other circumstances, he might be interested in dating her, but images of Hanna, sexy and naked, danced through his mind.

He shook his head, smiling.

"I'll have to pass. I don't like the idea of you driving my students away. Anyway, I'm already seeing someone."

It wasn't exactly a lie. He wanted to be seeing Hanna. He wanted to be doing more than seeing her.

Hanna stood in the atrium, books cradled against her chest, staring at the stairway with the dark blue metal railings. Room 204. Up that stairway and to the right.

She watched other people walking up the stairs, most going to classes on the second floor. Like "Psychology for the Businesswoman" or "Changing Lifestyles Reflected in Pop Culture" or "Learn to Crochet" or "Writing the Short Story" . . . or a dozen other fascinating courses she could have signed up for. And some people were going to "Kama Sutra for the Beginner."

She glanced at her watch. The class started in twenty minutes. She didn't have to go up right now. She drummed her fingers on the course book. *Kama Sutra: The Art of Loving,* by Jeremy Smith. Although she had told Grey she wasn't going to take the course, she'd reconsidered, thinking long and hard about the reasons she had used to convince herself not to go.

The fact that her sister knew the instructor made it a bit weird. Not that the two of them would discuss her—*of course they wouldn't*—but the whole thing made Hanna uncomfortable. But that was a minor concern.

Then there was the embarrassment factor. Since the course was primarily about the Kama Sutra, the instructor would probably discuss sexual positions—how could he not?—and that would be weird and awkward if she was there alone. Even if she wasn't alone, actually. Also, the course covered not just Kama Sutra but other areas of sexual awakening, too, including Tantra and other techniques. That was the main reason Grey had chosen it. True, the issue of a woman not achieving orgasm was only one of the topics to be covered, but since she was a single woman in the class, people might figure out why she was there.

But the most important reason was that every minute she sat in the course she would think about the fact that she had intended to take it with Grey. It would be a constant reminder of the relationship she and Grey had shared—and the fact that they were no longer together.

She missed Grey coming in the door at 6:20 every evening, dropping his bag by the door, then dragging her into his arms as if he couldn't wait to hold her. The way he'd called her every day during the afternoon lull at work, just wanting to say hi—but she'd known it was so much more than that. He'd adored her. He'd delighted in being with her.

If only he had loved her.

She stared at the book she had cradled in her arms. *The Art of Loving.* Grey certainly had made it an art with her. He had done everything he could to help her with her problem. When he'd made love to her, he'd kissed her long and lovingly, caressed her with great patience and tenderness. He'd bought books and tried techniques, loving her long into the night.

And even on nights when they hadn't made love, he

used to hold her close all night long. Her chest tightened. She missed that so much.

But he was not a part of her life now.

She stared at the book, knowing she needed to take control and solve her own problem. Other women had orgasms. There was no reason she shouldn't have them, too.

And she really wanted to have them.

Grace's suggestion hadn't worked. Hanna's cheeks burned as she remembered her salacious fling with a total stranger. No, actually a total stranger would have been a much better idea. She, on the other hand, had chosen someone who came into her shop on a regular basis. Someone whom, if she'd thought about it for half a second, she would have realized she would see again. And again.

He had come into the shop twice since the Incident. The first time, she had ducked away before he'd seen her. At least, she hoped he hadn't seen her. The second time, she hadn't spotted him in time and she'd glanced up from making a double latte with a sprinkle of cinnamon to see him standing right in front of her. He'd smiled, their gazes had locked, then she'd sputtered, made some ridiculous excuse—she couldn't remember what—and dove for the door to her office. Not the ideal way to treat him after stripping naked in front of him, then climbing onto his lap and fucking him silly.

She really needed to find another way to solve her problem. Maybe this course was the answer. That's why

Grey had signed her up for it. Just because they'd broken up didn't mean she shouldn't take the course.

She clung to the book and chewed her lower lip. But did she really want to sit in a classroom where sex was the topic of discussion? The course synopsis mentioned techniques, breathing, and exercises. What kind of exercises would they do? She could imagine a class full of people sitting on mats on the floor breathing heavily. Would they work with partners? Would the instructor actually show them, or have them practice, specific positions? Since she didn't have a partner, would the instructor partner with her? Of course he wouldn't do that . . . any of it. But what if he did?

And what about the instructor? According to his biography, he'd done research on various sexual disciplines and techniques, including Kama Sutra and Tantric sex, and he had written several books on the topic. Also, he'd studied Reiki energy healing and other New Age topics. No wonder he and her sister got along so well.

He was essentially an expert on sex. And a mystic. The guy could probably look into her eyes and *know* her problem on first sight.

She sucked in a breath. Oh, God, she couldn't do this.

She spun around and lurched forward—and ran smack into a hard, male chest. She backed away from the buttons pressed against her nose and glanced up.

Her heart raced into high gear. Her mystery date from the coffee shop.

"Hello." J.M. watched Hanna, hoping she wouldn't flee to the door before he could talk to her. Then he saw the book she was carrying. His book. The latest he'd written, and the one he'd be using as a text for the course.

"You're taking the Kama Sutra course?" he asked.

"Oh, uh . . ." She glanced at the copy of the same book he held in his hand. "Well, I was going to, but . . . I think . . . I'm not going to after all."

"That's too bad. I've been told it's very helpful. Why did you change your mind?"

"The only reason I was going to take it is because my boyfriend . . ." Her gaze met his, widened, then ricocheted away. "I mean, my ex-boyfriend, he signed me up. We're not together anymore, so . . ."

He smiled. So he had a chance with her after all. "You don't need a partner to go."

She clutched his book tight against her bosom and he remembered how soft those full, round breasts were against his naked chest. How smooth and silky to the touch. And how the nipples felt in his mouth. His cock stirred.

"Oh, I know. It's just that . . ."

She glanced up at him from beneath her long eyelashes with an almost coquettish look, though he doubted she intended it. She leaned a little closer. The scent of jasmine, rose, and vanilla tickled his senses, sending a vivid image of her sitting on his lap, his cock buried deep inside her.

"I don't think I'll be comfortable. You know, a single woman sitting in a classroom where everyone is talking about sex." She spoke quietly, as though sharing a secret.

"Well, I doubt *everyone* will be talking about sex."

She shrugged. "The instructor will be and he seems . . . very knowledgeable."

He grinned. "Isn't that a good thing?"

She nodded. "Sure, but it can be a little intimidating, too."

Clearly, it wouldn't be wise to tell her he was the instructor of the Kama Sutra course. At least, not right now. Although he didn't like hiding his identity, it would only embarrass her.

He could sense that this fascinating woman craved sexual excitement and desperately wanted to experience the awe of ecstasy, but she was limited by her own inhibitions. The night of their delightful encounter, she had somehow pushed past those inhibitions. Briefly. What he had assumed was a wild, carefree romp on her part had actually been a momentous step forward.

He would bet she'd never achieved an orgasm in a man's arms and that had motivated her enough to push her boundaries. She had thought she might find what she needed with a stranger. With one brief fling. But that wouldn't do it. She needed more. With a patient, loving partner.

He was prepared to be that partner. To guide her and help her discover what would bring her bliss.

But first, he'd have to convince her not to run away. From him. Or from herself . . . and her deepest desires.

Hanna watched his gaze grow intense, as though he was coming to some conclusion about her. Probably that she was a slut monkey, but she knew that was ridiculous. He would have decided she was a slut monkey the moment she'd torn off her clothes and thrown herself at him.

She glanced at her watch. Six fifty.

"I should be going. Nice seeing you again." Her face flushed as she thought about how much she'd seen last time.

So maybe "nice" wasn't quite accurate, since seeing him tonight had dredged up the whole embarrassing incident again. Still, he was good to look at and, as embarrassing as the incident was, it was certainly fodder for many erotic daydreams.

She turned to leave.

"Wait."

Reluctantly, she turned toward him again.

"I can tell you're embarrassed by what happened between us the other night."

Her cheeks flushed hotly.

"I want you to know that I was hoping you'd be there that night. I wanted to see you. I wanted to ask you out."

"Really?"

She understood that any man would jump into the game if a strange woman tore her clothes off in front of him and demanded sex. It was in their makeup. But to know he'd actually been attracted to her before the deed made her feel infinitely better.

"Yes. And I still want to." He smiled.

He had the most gorgeous smile. All white teeth and dimples.

He glanced at the clock high on the wall. "Class is going to start in a minute, so I've got to get up there. But would you meet me back here afterward? Say, nine fifteen?"

She drew in a breath, confusing emotions swirling through her brain. She liked him . . . but she'd recently broken up with Grey . . . but she'd had sex with this man.

She realized that last one was actually a pro, not a con. She already knew what to expect. No awkwardness about that first-date kiss, or when was the right time to go all the way. If she met him tonight then, conceivably, tonight could be the right time.

She sucked in an unsteady breath at the thought of that delicious but unsettling possibility.

"Hanna, please say yes. Meet me here?"

She stared at him, hesitant.

"I don't even know your name."

"That's easy to fix. My name is . . . J.M."

He held out his hand in offer of a handshake. She placed her hand in his, loving the feel of his big fingers wrapped around hers.

"J.M.?"

"My parents named me after my two grandfathers, and instead of picking one name over the other, they always just called me J.M." He smiled. "So, what do you say?"

Slowly, she withdrew her hand from the warmth of his. She nodded, more because of his compelling brown eyes than anything else. Gazing into their depths, she could feel his sincerity. He didn't just want her because she'd been available. His attraction to her felt tangible—like a soft light shining on her, filling her with warmth.

"Well, I do have some work to do at the café."

His smile broadened.

"Great. Do you want me to meet you there?"

"No," she answered a little abruptly. The thought of being alone with him again, at the scene of the crime, so to speak, unnerved her. "I'll meet you here."

Grey stepped into the classroom and moved up the middle aisle between the neat rows of tables and chairs to the center of the room, then selected a chair two in from the aisle. He sat down and glanced around. Several men and women sat in pairs around the room, and there were a few other individuals.

He pushed his flat leather case forward on the desk in front of him and stared at the blackboard.

Hanna wasn't here. He had hoped she would decide to come after all. He still cursed himself for how he had handled things with Hanna.

He had fallen in love with her early in the relationship, and that love had deepened throughout their year together. He'd wanted to be with her always, to marry her. But he'd known it wouldn't be fair to her. She wouldn't want . . . No woman would want to marry a man like him. So he'd held off telling her the truth about himself so he could enjoy their relationship just a little bit longer.

He loved her, and he'd wanted it to last as long as possible, but he knew, one day, he would have to tell her the truth and they would break up.

As stupid as it seemed now, he hadn't been able to tell her about his problem the night she told him she loved him, because he knew it would be the end of the road for them.

But the pain of being without her burned through him. He loved her and she loved him, and he realized he had to take a chance. Maybe they could figure out a way to make their relationship work.

He had decided to tell her everything. How he was

sterile after a childhood disease. And even though he knew she wanted a family, he loved her with all his heart and wanted her back. He intended to do everything possible to convince her they were right for each other, and then they could figure out what to do about the future.

But before he did any of that, he had to win back her heart.

He pulled out a pen and paper from his briefcase.

As for Hanna's problem in the bedroom, it wasn't her fault. She was sexy and alluring. She made his heart pound and his body tighten just being near him.

Whatever the reason, he would figure it out. This course would provide him with tools so he could help her.

If she ever let him into her bed again. And, more important, into her heart.

He hoped she would let him stay at her place once a week when he was in town for the course. That way, they could get to know each other again, a courtship of sorts. And when the time was right, he would sweep her into his arms and tell her the truth. Then she'd have to decide the fate of their relationship all over again. But at least this time, she'd have the facts straight.

He drummed his fingers on the desk and glanced at the clock at the front of the room. Two minutes after seven.

A tall, clean-shaven guy with longish but tidy hair,

wearing black denim jeans and a long-sleeved black shirt, walked into the room and strode to the front, then smiled at the class.

"Good evening. My name is Jeremy Smith and this course is 'Kama Sutra for the Beginner.'"

He turned to the blackboard and wrote his name, then the course name.

"In this course, we will explore the Kama Sutra as a guide to spiritual bliss. We will also discuss the sacred practice of Tantric sex. Don't let the words 'spiritual' and 'sacred' throw you. We will be studying specific techniques and practices you can use in your own sex life to bring more joy to your, and your lover's, life. We'll also take a look at some common problems people have in their sex lives and discuss possible solutions or courses of action. Of course, I have also provided a recommended reading list for those of you who are interested."

He leaned against the edge of the desk in a relaxed pose.

"I know that sex is a sensitive topic and some of you might find it difficult to raise your hand and ask questions in a public setting, though I hope as the course goes on you'll start to feel more comfortable. For those of you who do have questions but would like to talk to me on an individual basis, see me after class and we can arrange a time. I want everyone to get the most they can out of this course."

He smiled, then turned to his desk and pulled out some books from his bag.

This Jeremy seemed like a friendly enough guy. Approachable. That was great. After class, Grey intended to talk to him about Hanna's problem and see if he'd be willing to give Grey a little extra guidance.

four

Hanna snapped the red elastic band around the pile of envelopes on her desk—all the paychecks ready for her staff on Friday morning. She glanced at her watch—8:45. She had all her paperwork done, including all of Monday morning's orders ready to go.

She glanced around, drumming her fingers on the desktop. It wouldn't hurt to head over to the university a little early. She'd only have to wait five minutes or so, plus the time it would take everyone to get out of the classroom. Or, at least, how long it would take J.M. to leave the classroom.

She thought about his long, warm fingers stroking her skin as he had that night in the café. Her cheeks burned again at how brazen she'd been, and second thoughts about meeting him cascaded through her brain—but she wanted to see him again. And she couldn't live her life hiding out here in her office.

She dropped her face into her hands. *Oh, God, I still can't believe I threw myself at him like that.*

She sighed, knowing the man would surely seek her out. He seemed genuinely interested in her, not just pursuing her because she was *easy*. Remembering the warmth of his gaze and the sincerity in his eyes, she knew she would go and meet him. She wanted to see where this might lead.

She grabbed her purse from her drawer and stood up. As she headed out the door, then locked it behind her, she wondered at the irony of the situation. Grey had signed her up for this course, yet rather than helping them with their sex life, it was allowing her to hook up with another man.

Great. She stuffed her keys in her purse. Now she felt guilty, too.

J.M. glanced at the line of students in front of his desk. At least seven.

He smiled at the bouncy redhead and her boyfriend as they thanked him for his suggestions for books about sexual fantasies, then he glanced at the clock on the wall. Nine fifteen. How long would Hanna wait for him, given her already skittish frame of mind? Would she have second thoughts and leave? Or worse, would she assume he'd stood her up?

Sure, she'd probably be okay waiting another ten minutes or so, but . . . His gaze strayed to the man in the business suit carrying a notebook and pen, clearly ready with a list of questions. Behind him stood a young man with shoulder-length hair in the unkempt style so popular with university students these days. He carried a stack of books from J.M.'s suggested reading list for the course, probably wanting to discuss some of the finer details of what he'd read. Next stood two young women chatting and giggling, glancing at J.M. slyly, probably hoping to shock him with some kind of proposition like asking him to join them in a ménage à trois. It had happened before. A few others stood behind them.

From the look of things, he might be a half hour or more.

And then there was the tall, broad-shouldered man with sandy brown hair in the denim jacket hanging back, obviously waiting to talk to him privately. That usually meant a sensitive topic to discuss—something J.M. couldn't just blow off until another time. Not that J.M. would ever blow off his students—but he could defer them.

This man—Grey something-or-other, J.M. recalled from the introductions—had a determined set to his jaw. Whatever he wanted to discuss with J.M., it was important to him. J.M. realized he could definitely be here for a while.

Hanna glanced at her watch again. Twenty minutes late. Being that late didn't seem consistent with the behavior of a man who claimed to be interested in her. Not that she was a stickler for punctuality—she wasn't always on time herself—but it wasn't like he had to come from across town. He only had to walk the length of a hall and down a stairway.

The instructor might have kept them late, but this was longer than she'd expect. Unless it was a really fabulous class and they had all lost track of the time.

Maybe she should have taken the class after all.

She glanced at her watch again. Maybe she'd just go up to the classroom and take a look. She'd been reluctant to do so earlier, for no good reason. So it was a class about Kama Sutra? That shouldn't make her feel odd hanging around outside the room.

She glanced toward the stairway, which had been teeming with students only twenty minutes earlier as the various second-floor classes had let out. Over the past ten minutes, only the occasional person had strolled by.

Hanna jogged up the stairs, turned right, then passed Room 207 on the left . . . then 206 on the right. . . . Up ahead she noticed 204, the room listed on her course confirmation.

She approached the room and noticed the door was open. She peered inside.

Grey waited patiently as the last person in line, a tall, slim brunette in tight jeans and a loose red sweater, moved toward the instructor. As they began their discussion, a woman's voice snatched Grey's gaze toward the door.

"Excuse me, are you almost finished in here?" Framed in the doorway was a tall, athletic-looking woman wearing coveralls, her jet-black hair tied back in a ponytail. She held a large ring of keys that jangled together as she swung them back and forth.

The instructor glanced toward her.

"We'll be done in a few minutes."

"Okay, I'll be back in ten." The custodian turned and strolled away.

Grey glanced at the clock on the wall and realized it was getting late. He had wanted to call Hanna tonight—maybe drop in on her—but he might not get the chance. She liked to get up early on Wednesday mornings to run with her sister, so she wouldn't appreciate him calling too late. And he didn't want to do anything to annoy her.

He glanced at his watch, debating whether to abandon his effort to talk to the instructor in favor of dashing out to call Hanna.

"May I help you?"

Grey glanced at the instructor and realized the young woman who'd been last in line had left.

"Yes, actually." He stepped forward, clearing his throat, trying to figure out how to put his request to this stranger into words.

Hanna peered around the empty classroom in a daze. Everyone was gone. Even the instructor.

Had J.M. stood her up?

Her gaze wandered to the blackboard and for the first time she saw the big letters printed neatly in white chalk.

Kama Sutra for the Beginner
Moved to Room 216

That room was down the other end of the hall. She turned around and headed out the door, then turned left.

"A little late, aren't you?"

She stopped in her tracks at the sound of Grey's teasing voice. Her gaze shot to him as he strolled toward her from a few yards on the other side of the stairway. He stared at her with intense yet sexy dark green eyes, his gaze softened by the way his lips curled up in a sensuous grin. Awareness prickled through her, as it always did when she was near him—a gentle blush of heat that took her breath away.

Her gaze flickered over his wavy, sandy brown hair, the arched eyebrows that accentuated his dark eyes, then continued down his classic nose to his full lips and strong jaw, shadowed by a light growth of beard.

"What are you doing here?" she asked.

His denim jacket emphasized his broad shoulders and his jeans hugged his long, lean legs. He was taller than J.M. by a couple of inches and, as he drew closer, she felt an overwhelming urge to rush into his arms, to feel the solid comfort of his embrace.

She shifted her gaze to his and, to her dismay, still saw

the glow of love in his eyes. An illusion that had once fooled her into believing he actually loved her. Even knowing it was an illusion, the sight sent a quiver of emotion through her.

"I came for the class. What about you?"

He stood only a yard away now, his closeness triggering a growing warmth within her.

The surge of emotion reminded her just how much she'd missed him. And just how much she loved him.

She glanced around guiltily, worried that J.M. would appear at any moment. Not that she shouldn't be going out with someone else—after all, she and Grey had broken up—but she didn't want to be obvious about it. She knew Grey wouldn't be happy about it and she didn't want to hurt him.

She stepped back into the classroom so that they wouldn't be visible if J.M. came down the hall. Grey followed her.

"I came to meet someone."

His mouth flattened into a thin line and she was sure he'd figured out the someone was a male.

"I really hoped you'd come to the class. It would have been a good experience for you."

She nodded. "I know. I almost did, but . . ." She shrugged. How could she explain she just wasn't comfortable with the idea? Maybe if they were still together, but taking the course with him now would be too strange.

She couldn't believe he had traveled all the way from New York for the course. Did he really intend to do that every week?

She thought about just how strange it would have been if she had decided earlier this evening to attend the course after all—with Grey *and* J.M. both in the class.

Her cheeks burned.

"Look, do you want to grab a coffee?" he asked. "I'd really like to talk to you."

She pursed her lips. "I'm sorry, I can't. I told you, I'm—"

"Right, you're meeting someone. A male someone, I presume."

She nodded, wishing she could have avoided confirming it.

He frowned. "Okay, I'm still in town tomorrow, so maybe I can give you a call."

"Of course. I . . ." She heard someone coming down the hall and she worried it was J.M. She really couldn't handle the two of them meeting right now. It would be way too awkward. "I really have to go."

"So I don't run into him. Okay, I'll call you tomorrow." He leaned forward and kissed her on the cheek.

The brief contact sent a sweeping rage of heated emotions washing through her. Her heart ached, loving him so much but knowing they weren't right for each other.

Her head understood it. Why couldn't her heart? And her hormones?

J.M. hurried down the hall toward the stairs. With the arrival of the custodian, he'd had a good excuse to shut things down early with his student Grey Bennet. But he hadn't. As it turned out, Grey had decided to set an appointment to talk the next day, so it had all worked out. Except after J.M. had packed up all his books and course materials, he'd had to track down the custodian to lock the door.

To his surprise, he saw Hanna standing at the top of the stairs glancing down toward the lower floor.

"Hanna, sorry I'm late."

Hanna's gaze darted from the back of Grey's tall form, as he continued down the stairs to the hallway on the main level, to J.M. as he strode toward her.

He smiled broadly. "I'm glad you waited. Were you looking for me in the classroom?"

"Yes. I saw the note on the board—about the classroom change. I thought I'd wait here a few minutes."

If J.M. had arrived a moment earlier, he would have seen Grey kissing her just before he'd headed down the stairs. Her heart hammered in her chest. Thank heavens that awkward moment had been avoided.

"So where would you like to go? Do you want to grab a coffee somewhere?" J.M. asked.

The thought of taking him back to the Hot Spot

Café conjured X-rated images of them making love in the corner.

"No. I don't think so." She didn't want to take him back to her place, either, since Grey just might decide to show up. "It's kind of late for a movie, and we couldn't really talk then anyway."

"We could watch a movie at my place," J.M. suggested. "I'm not too far away and I have one of the movies suggested in the course materials—if you're interested."

Ordinarily, she wouldn't go to a guy's apartment on a first date but, well, they had already had sex. And, as she became distinctly aware of his broad, masculine body close to hers, her gaze strayed to his big, strong hands and memories of them touching her, of the pleasure they'd given her, careened through her.

She glanced at his face, her gaze lingering on his full, sexy lips, and heat blossomed through her at the memory of him kissing her. Her mouth, her breasts, and . . . He had wanted to kiss her down there, but she had stopped him. Her sex flooded at the thought of his mouth warming her opening with tender kisses and strokes of his tongue.

Oh, man, she wanted him again. She wanted to see his big cock again, to feel it in her mouth. She wanted to feel his tongue lapping over her clit.

She couldn't believe this. Mere moments after Grey had kissed her, here she was drooling over another man.

Why am I feeling guilty? Grey is my ex-boyfriend. A new man might be just what I need to get over him.

"Or we could do something else." J.M.'s words broke her reverie.

"No, going to your place would be fine."

He smiled. "Great. Do you have a car here?"

"No, I walk. My place is just a couple of blocks away."

"Okay, mine's parked in C Lot."

They strolled down the stairs and out the side door toward the parking lot on the east side of the building. He stopped beside a small sleek silver Prius, one of the hybrids she'd been wishing for because they were so good for the environment. Unfortunately, it was still a little too pricey for her budget. He opened the door for her and she climbed inside. It was surprisingly roomy and she was amazed at how quiet the engine was as he drove across the parking lot, then out onto the street.

Watching the built-in GPS display their route helped divert her attention from her hot, hungry yearning for the sexy man beside her. Barely.

After about fifteen minutes of driving, he pulled into the driveway of a quaint century-old stone house in the upscale Birmingham district. He opened her door, then led her along the front path past the flowering bushes to the house. As he unlocked the door, anticipation curled through her. Soon she would be alone with him.

Inside, he flicked on a light to reveal rich wooden paneling and glossy hardwood floors.

"Nice place." She stroked her hand over the carved

wood wainscoting, itching to feel something hard under her fingertips.

"Thanks. It was a great find. I'm renting from a professor who's away on a year sabbatical—in Jerusalem, I think. Some kind of religious studies."

He led her down a long hall, past the kitchen on the left, to a large living room with a big picture window. The moon, which was almost full, cast soft light on a small but well-maintained backyard with a stone patio surrounded by a lovely garden. Tall bushes encircled the yard, providing privacy.

He pulled a movie from a large collection of DVDs on a dark-stained bookshelf beside the high-definition TV. But she didn't have movies on her mind. As he turned around, she stepped toward him and rested her hands on his chest, then stroked his shoulders.

This might be a desperate attempt to distract herself from the lingering feelings that seeing Grey had stirred up, but it felt right . . . and she wanted it so badly.

At the feel of her hands on him, J.M. wrapped his arms around her and drew her against him. It was heaven feeling her warm, feminine body pressed the length of his.

Her hands glided up to his cheeks, cupping them gently in her palms. She tipped her head up and gazed into his eyes with a longing that accelerated his heartbeat. He settled his mouth on hers with gentle precision. Her arms slid around his neck, and her lips moved under his, soft and giving. His tongue speared into her mouth and she murmured her approval.

He pulled her tighter to his body, feeling a tide of desire wash through him. Her breasts pressed against his chest and her nipples hardened into tight beads, burning into him. His groin tightened in response and he felt himself expand.

He responded to her far too quickly. With his discipline, his experience, his will, he could delay an erection for hours, yet this woman had him hungering for her within minutes.

He hadn't expected this. He'd intended to let the evening unfold like a regular first date.

Her soft sigh quivered through him. She snuggled closer, her hands gliding down his chest, around his waist, then cupping his buttocks. He hadn't expected to make love to her tonight. In fact, he'd promised himself he wouldn't. But it seemed she had other ideas.

Which suited him fine. It just wouldn't be quite what she expected.

He drew his lips from hers and gazed into her eyes.

"You weren't able to come to orgasm last time. Has that always been a problem?"

She glanced at him uncomfortably.

"Yes," she said quietly.

He turned her hands over and caressed her palms with

his lips, knowing his breath, along with the gentle pressure of his mouth, sent her senses reeling.

"This course tonight . . . it's not my first one." He wanted to be careful not to scare her away with his expertise. "I have studied Tantra along with various other disciplines over the years. Part of the Tantric practice is that a man holds off ejaculating for hours . . . days . . . even months."

"Really?" Her eyes widened.

"I can stay erect for long periods of time." He stroked her shoulders and smiled. "Which means I can concentrate exclusively on you. I can help you focus on your own body and find what works for you." He gazed into her eyes with hot intensity. "You'll find that there are different levels of orgasm. Deliciously mild to mind-numbing in their intensity. There are spiritual levels you can reach that defy the progression of normal time. You can feel your consciousness expand beyond the physical to the realm of eternity."

He longed to take her there, to that place of infinite bliss. And he knew, with her, he wouldn't be far behind.

When she answered, her voice came out husky. "I'd be happy to come just once. Just a regular orgasm. Do you really think you can . . . you know . . . get me there?"

He smiled and drew her hand to his lips, then kissed each knuckle. "Absolutely." He stroked her wrist with the tip of his thumb and she shivered. "But not tonight."

"What? Why not?" she asked.

"I want to show you the pleasure of touch. Of intimacy without orgasm."

She rolled her eyes. "I know that already."

"Ah, but only with frustration. I mean without orgasm as a goal. I want to touch and stroke you all over, but with no thought of anything beyond the sensual experience itself. Are you game?"

Hanna stared at him, her eyes drifting to his sensual mouth. A mouth she longed to kiss again and again.

"I . . . uh . . . guess so." She couldn't say no, but she wasn't quite sure what she was agreeing to. "So we're going to make love, but not try for an orgasm?"

He shook his head. "No making love. Just touching." He smiled. "Me touching you. Stroking you. Making you feel pleasure."

Would he really just touch her, then not make love to her? If things heated up, wouldn't he want to?

"In fact, I promised myself tonight I wouldn't make love to you. I want you to know that I don't want you just for sex. After our first encounter, I don't think you really believe that."

"Oh." It was true. After she'd thrown herself at him in her full naked glory, how could she think anything else?

She'd been lucky he had walked into her café that night—that he had been the one she'd tried being wild and crazy on.

He unbuttoned his shirt and slipped it off his shoulders,

revealing his broad, muscular chest. Her fingers itched to stroke over his smooth flesh. He began to unbuckle his belt and she felt a quiver start in her belly and ripple through her entire body as the zipper slid down and the pants dropped to the floor, revealing his black briefs, and his member straining to be free of them.

That, too, she longed to touch.

"If we're not making love, why are you getting undressed?"

"To make you more comfortable."

Was he kidding?

He dropped his briefs to the floor and she licked her lips at the sight of his long, hard erection.

She began to unfasten the buttons of her blouse, but he stepped forward and gently grasped her hands. He drew them to his lips and kissed first one palm, then the other, sending spirals of electricity coiling through her.

"My dearest Hanna, would you allow me to remove your clothes, then touch and stroke your beautiful body?"

The formal way he asked to do such wickedly exciting things thrilled her.

She simply nodded, unable to find her voice.

His fingers caressed along the neckline of her blouse, then dipped into the fabric to release the first button, with a touch as light as the brush of a butterfly's wing. He released the next, then the next, thrilling her senses with his delicate touch. Finally, her blouse gaped open and he stroked it over her shoulders. It dropped to the floor in a heap. He stroked along the lace edging of her bra, then between her breasts. He released the front clasp and reverently drew the cups aside.

His look of awe nearly melted her heart.

"You are exquisite."

His heated gaze grazed her breasts, and her nipples puckered shamelessly. She longed for him to touch them, but he didn't. He merely took in the sight of them. Finally, he unzipped her jeans and slid them down her hips. She stepped out of them, now wearing only her pink ankle socks and skimpy black panties. He hooked his fingers under the lacy elastic and drew them down, then off. Now naked, except for her little pink socks, she felt alluring yet somehow innocent, like a schoolgirl.

He gazed down at them and smiled, as though having the same thoughts.

He took her hand and led her across the living room and into his bedroom. The king-sized bed seemed appropriate for his size. A broad, tall man needed a big bed.

He rolled the navy and forest green paisley duvet down to reveal cream sheets and pillowcases with a navy ribbon edging. She sat down, and the high-quality cotton sheets felt like silk against her skin. He tossed aside two of the pillows and moved the remaining two to the center of the bed.

"Why don't you lie on your stomach?" he suggested.

She settled onto her stomach, tucking one pillow under her chin and pushing the other aside. He sat down beside her and his hands began moving over her back in long, soothing strokes. Relaxing, rhythmic circles . . . up the center of her back, across her shoulders, then down to her hips . . . then up the center again. She found herself relaxing under his sure touch.

"Does the reason you signed up for the Kama Sutra course have anything to do with the fact that some of the subject material deals with women having trouble coming to orgasm?"

"Yes, my ex noticed the course and thought that it might help."

His fingertips feathered out from her spine with a gentle pressure; then he stroked over her shoulders and down her arms, his fingers moving back and forth, kneading her muscles. Her cares drifted away as he paid careful attention to her arms, then her wrists and hands.

"As I mentioned earlier, I have studied Tantra, so I know a little about this. Women have a great capacity for orgasm. There are many different types of female orgasm, like clitoral, vaginal, G-spot."

He lightly kneaded each finger in turn.

"There are also ejaculatory . . . anal . . . and there are orgasms that are a blend of two or more of these."

She sighed at the wonder of so many ways to have pleasure.

"And for each type, a woman can have multiple orgasms."

"That's amazing," she murmured. It was also amazing

how he'd turned her body into a boneless mass of jelly.

He shifted to her thighs, then kneaded his way down her legs to her ankles, then did long, light strokes up and down. Her limbs grew limp.

"But the only way you can have an orgasm is if you allow yourself to. If you're not having orgasms, it's because for some reason, you won't allow yourself to have the pleasure."

She sighed, as much from the pleasure of his touch as from his words. "I know, I'm supposed to relax."

"That's the answer most people give, but it's not easy to do."

Finally, someone who understood.

"The real question is, why are you afraid to let loose?"

He slipped off one of her socks, then the other. Now that her socks were gone, she became intensely aware of her nakedness.

"Maybe deep down you feel guilt or shame about the idea of having sex—or of enjoying it. Maybe something else is going on."

Shame? But she knew there was nothing wrong with having sex.

Didn't she?

He began working on her feet in a deliriously wonderful foot rub.

Every part of her tingled under the expert pressure of his fingertips. As he moved up her legs again, she felt a prickly awareness of his masculinity . . . of his nudity . . . of hers. He caressed her bare buttocks, his palms stroking and soothing but at the same time exhilarating her naked flesh.

His hands moved round and round.

She was aware of her buttocks squeezing together, then parting slightly with every circular stroke. Her vagina pulsed with heat. She longed for him to slip his fingers between her legs and stroke her there.

His fingers slid down the slope of her buttocks to her thighs and she moaned softly.

J.M. felt his cock harden at the soft sound she made. He wanted her to get used to his touch and for her to associate it with being in a relaxed state. At the same time, he wanted to slip his finger inside her and stir her sexual arousal to a frantic state, then flip her over and thrust into her until they both wailed in ecstasy.

"Tantra teaches ways to get past the problems of mental or emotional distractions." He dragged his hands down her legs.

"Like what?"

He massaged her feet some more.

He stroked up the side of her leg, then over her hip.

"Why don't you roll over?"

As she rolled onto her back, he grasped the pillow and repositioned it under her head. She lay there, staring up at him, her body beautiful in its nakedness.

"It teaches you how to be aware of your breathing—slow and deep at first, then growing more rapid as excitement builds."

Her look of disappointment told him she wasn't very impressed with that idea. Newcomers often didn't realize the power of breath.

Her breasts pointed straight to the ceiling, the nipples fully erect. Her soft golden pubic hair curled daintily between her thighs as her long, shapely legs lay parted in her relaxed state.

His cock twitched. He dearly wanted to capture those nipples in his mouth, to feel them pebble and distend as he sucked and kneaded them until she wailed in orgasm. He loved bringing a woman to orgasm by touching her breasts alone—and he was determined to show Hanna that particular pleasure at some point.

He stroked over her shoulders and down her arms, then back to her shoulders.

"While you're making love . . ." He swirled his fingertips around her breasts, not touching them, then stroked her ribs, then back up to her shoulders. ". . . or masturbating . . ." His fingertips danced along her collarbone. He could feel her sexual tension heighten as he caressed her. ". . . concentrate on the pleasure you feel."

Finally, he stroked over her breasts, lightly, her beaded nipples caressing his palms, then up to her shoulders.

Her hands clutched at the sheets, her fingers crumpling the fabric. He continued swirling his hands around her breasts, then over them . . . around, then over.

He repeated the path, stroking over those lovely mounds like they were any other part of her body. Of course, every part of her body was an erotic, tempting treat.

Her nipples pushed into his hands every time he stroked over them.

"Wrap yourself in the delightful sensations of your body."

Slowly, her fingers relaxed, the fabric slipping from her hands.

He stroked down the center of her chest to her navel, then out to her hips, then back up. He caressed the underside of her breasts with his fingertips.

He stroked each leg, from her hip to her ankle, then up again. After several moments on her legs, he applied his attention to her feet again, calming her to a deeper level of relaxation.

"Make sounds that reflect your pleasure and move your body as feels natural."

When he stroked upward to her inner thighs and brushed lightly against her folds, she moaned and arched a little. His fingertips glided down to her knees, then up again.

"If you're with a partner, think about how much you love being with that person and how much pleasure he is giving you."

She parted her legs more, opening to him.

"Don't let your mind be distracted away from that pleasure."

He had to use all of his willpower not to accept her invitation and stroke over her glistening slit. He'd love nothing better than to prowl over her and drive his aching cock into her wet passage and thrust his way to heaven. Nothing except to help her find her way there first.

He stroked lightly over her labia, staying to the outer folds, then downward again, building her sexual energy.

"Most women find it easiest to orgasm with clitoral stimulation." He stroked upward again, then over her folds. "The clitoris, whose sole purpose is pleasure, is extremely sensitive to touch."

His fingertips slid between the folds.

"The tip is too sensitive for a lot of direct pressure, so it's better to stimulate around the clitoris at first . . ." He found the tiny bud, then spiraled around. ". . . experimenting with different strokes, varying pressure and speed."

Her soft, breathy murmurs quivered through him.

"Fingers are not as sensitive as the tissue around the clitoris, so it is better to use mouth and tongue to stimulate it."

He eased her legs apart and leaned toward her intimate flesh. He drew the folds apart with his thumbs and dabbed his tongue against the little point of flesh. Her body quivered beneath him. He licked the sides with delicate strokes of his tongue, sometimes dabbing the tip.

Her fingers tangled in his hair and she moaned in pleasure, but he could feel her muscles tightening.

He tilted his head up and gazed at her.

"The first inch or two of the vaginal opening has the most nerve endings so is the most sensitive part. Once a woman is very aroused . . ." He slid his fingers inside her. ". . . she finds it very pleasurable when stroked there. . . ." He licked her clit again. "Especially while her partner continues to stimulate her clitoris." He leaned down and licked her again. She moaned and arched her pelvis upward. He quivered his tongue against her clit while stroking her inside.

At this point, he did not vary the way he stroked her vagina. The way he was doing it was clearly giving her great pleasure.

"A man needs to remember that once he finds a stroke or movement that works, he should keep doing it . . . exactly the same way. Many men think they should keep doing more and more. More speed . . . More pressure . . . More movement . . ." He licked her clit again. "But as long as it's working, he should just keep doing the same thing."

He swirled his tongue around her clit, his fingers continuing to stroke gently inside her.

Her gasps and moans told him she was approaching orgasm, but he could feel the tension in her tightening muscles.

He fluttered his tongue on her button and she sucked

in a sharp breath. Her legs, limp and relaxed only a few moments before, were stiff and tense. He slowed the strokes of his tongue and his fingers. Slowly, her legs relaxed and he could feel the tension ease from her.

He stroked her with his hands from neck to ankle, soothing her. Her body was thrumming with unreleased sexual energy. He returned to her feet and gently kneaded them until she sighed.

"Hanna, I'd love to show you a Tantric breathing exercise."

He held out his hand to her.

"Breathing?" Hanna took his hand and drew herself up, disappointed at the direction he was taking things. She doubted breathing was going to do anything for her.

He sat cross-legged on the bed and drew her toward him.

"Sit on my lap and wrap your legs around me," he directed.

She settled herself on his lap, then wrapped her legs around him. His long, hard penis trapped between their bodies sent heat melting through her. She wrapped her arms around him and he cuddled her close to his body, their cheeks touching. The warm, intimate embrace made her feel deeply cherished.

"This loving, intimate pose is called Kshiraniraka, or Milk and Water, in Kama Sutra. The same position is called YabYum in Tantric teachings. Notice that our heart chakras are touching, which allows a deep, loving energy to pass between us easily."

She'd heard her sister talk about chakras many times. Grace had told her there were seven major energy centers in the body, called chakras, spanning from the bottom of the torso to the top of the head.

"This position can be used as an embrace leading up to intercourse or it can be used after full penetration."

His cock twitched, sending a shiver through her. She'd love to experience full penetration right now.

"Controlled breathing is an important part of Tantric sex. There are many breathing exercises you can do, including changing the speed of your breathing to increase excitement or to keep you on the edge of sexual excitement by holding off an orgasm. What I want to do with you right now is to harmonize our breathing to raise the sexual energy between us.

"Draw in a breath of air . . . slow and deep. . . . Focus on the air traveling through your body, moving low into your belly."

She breathed in slowly. Deeper than usual, feeling her belly expand.

"Hold it for a moment. Then breathe out."

She exhaled slowly.

"Feel the air moving up through your body, then out."

She felt her belly contract and the air flow out her nostrils.

"Think of energy from the universe being drawn into you as you breathe in, and flowing down through your body, filling you with light. As you exhale, imagine all negativity and tension leaving your body with the ex-pelled air."

She felt a warmth filling her and a sense of peace.

"I'm going to match your breathing, inhaling when you exhale and exhaling when you inhale. This focused breathing helps build a high-energy charge that can be directed from the genitals through the entire body in a wave of energy called Kundalini."

As she breathed, she felt a warm sensation moving slowly through her body.

"Sacred sex helps you learn to have an orgasm in your whole body, not just here." His finger stroked the side of her mound, which was nestled against his cock. "It also helps you become multiorgasmic. With training, as your sexual excitement rises, you can move the sexual energy up through your body, through the chakras, transforming it until you attain mystical states of con-sciousness."

He slid his hand up her back as he spoke. Warmth expanded in waves along her spine.

"You are very lucky. In Tantra, to attain a higher state of bliss, a man holds off ejaculation over time to build sexual energy. A woman, on the other hand, builds this energy naturally. She is capable of reaching this blissful state every time."

His hand slid downward again, coming to rest on her lower back.

"Right now, I'd like you to pay attention to the energy in your sacral chakra. That's your sexual energy center."

He slid his hand between their bodies and placed it on her stomach, a couple of inches below her navel, matching where his hand lay on her back.

"It's right there. Think of the chakra as a large ball of light, spinning very fast. It is full of warm, golden light. Every time you breathe, you're filling it with more light."

She realized it felt quite warm where she imagined the ball of light and she noticed a strange stirring. Warm sensations soon turned hot and she felt full of yearning. Her intimate muscles tightened and she longed for his hard penis inside her.

She tightened her arms around him and leaned toward his ear.

"Make love to me, J.M. I want you inside me."

His cock swelled with need, demanding to be inside the warm embrace of her body, but with practiced concentration he stored the energy from his heightened arousal in his sacral chakra.

"Good. You're feeling the energy build in your chakra. Let it grow. Let it fill you."

The yearning became more intense. Involuntarily, she squeezed her intimate muscles, and almost gasped. Intense pleasure flooded through her. She squeezed again. A small moan escaped her lips.

He kissed her cheek.

"Wonderful, Hanna. Let the energy move through you," he encouraged. "Flutter your vaginal muscles."

She let go and the muscles in her internal passage fluttered as he'd suggested. Heat built within her sacral chakra, burning with an erotic intensity. She found herself rocking back and forth.

J.M.'s hands stroked up her spine. First one hand, then the other. Pleasure rose in waves, heating every part of her body. She moaned softly, letting it wash through her. J.M. continued stroking her and the heat moved upward through her body, pulsing at first, then building to a powerful stream that flooded up and outward. In that moment, she felt a deep clarity . . . almost as if she'd achieved a higher level of consciousness.

Then it slipped away.

J.M.'s arms encircled her and she felt wrapped in a delicious, blissful sense of well-being. He gently laid her down on the bed and cradled her against him.

five

The first thing Hanna became aware of when she woke up was a hot, hard body pressed against her back. The second thing was that she was thoroughly aroused.

Awareness prickled through her. Of her naked breast nestled into the warmth of J.M.'s hand. Of the feel of his breath caressing the back of her neck, sending tingles prancing along her spine. Of his hard body pressed against her, especially his hard cock nestled between her buttocks. She drew in a deep breath—which pushed her nipple firmly into his palm.

She lay still, wanting to linger in this delicious embrace. She gazed out the large window, watching clouds float across the vivid blue sky. Sunlight filled the room and birds twittered in the trees.

What a glorious day.

"Good morning," J.M. murmured in her ear, then kissed it.

As he nuzzled the base of her neck, electricity coursed through her. She sighed.

"Good morning."

It fell far short of what she wanted to say, but no words could convey the joy swirling through her. She just reveled in the closeness of this marvelous man. The man who had given her such a delightfully sensual experience last night.

An experience that left her wanting more. A *lot* more.

She rolled within his arms, then snuggled her cheek against his chest, the raspy hair tickling her nose. She kissed his satin-smooth flesh, then lightly nibbled his nipple. Dabbing with the tip of her tongue, she teased his nipple to a hard bead, then drew it into her mouth.

As she began to kiss down his stomach, he grasped her shoulders and drew her back up, then kissed her soundly. "You're not going to change my mind."

"What do you mean?" She gazed at him, feigning innocence.

"I said I wasn't going to make love to you."

"Last night," she added. "It's a new day."

Her hand slid around from his hip to his rapidly growing cock and she grasped it, then stroked lightly.

"That doesn't matter. It's still our first date."

He scooped up her hand and drew it to his lips, then kissed it delicately, sending her senses swirling.

"You obviously want to be inside me." She slid her

other hand to his cock and stroked under the head. "Why not let yourself?"

"Tell you what . . ." He grinned. "How about I give us what we both want . . . my cock inside you . . . but I won't make love to you?"

"Oh?" She slid her fingers around his hard cock and squeezed lightly, then stroked up and down. "And how exactly does that work?"

His hand joined hers on his cock, stroking with her, then shifted to the opening between her legs and dipped inside. She could feel her wetness as his fingers slid inside her with ease.

"Like this." He grasped his cock and pressed it to her folds, then eased forward, sliding inside her.

She moaned at the glorious feel of his long, hard cock gliding into her depths and stretching her.

She squeezed him, waiting for his first thrust.

And waiting.

His arms tightened around her waist as he drew her tight to his body and held her there.

She arched her pelvis, gaining an inch more depth.

"But we don't move," he said.

"Well, then how can we—?"

"We don't. The point is to share this loving intimacy for itself, without the goal of orgasm."

"What fun is that?"

He kissed the tip of her nose and laughed, a rumbling from deep within his chest.

"You are a delight."

He cuddled her close. She was aware of everywhere his body touched her. The ridges of his ribs against her breasts. The delicious feel of his raspy leg hair as his ankles tangled around hers. The steel-hard firmness of his muscular arms so warm around her arms and back.

She felt intensely cherished. And vulnerable . . . in a good way. Totally open to his strength—his cock a steel-hard muscle nestled inside her soft, feminine core.

She squeezed him again, her vagina embracing his masculine appendage, and tried not to think of it as a . . . cock. Hot and hard.

She tightened her arms around him, trying to pull him closer and deeper, but he was as deep as she could get him, without some cooperation on his part. So she eased away a little, then shifted forward, giving herself a little bit of a thrust. The walls of her vagina tingled and heat suffused her. She sucked in a deep breath.

"You're incorrigible." He flattened his hand on the small of her back and held her still. "Just relax."

Relax? Usually people said that when talking about trying to achieve orgasm, not avoid it. What was it with him?

But she realized he was very caring. Putting aside his own needs to satisfy hers. Because, ultimately, he seemed to believe this was a step to helping her find her O. Also, it made it clear he was a man of his word.

Her thoughts turned to last night and the unusual experience she'd had in his arms. Right after, she'd thought she had experienced an orgasm, but now she wasn't so sure. It wasn't the way other people described an orgasm. J.M. had talked about energy orgasms, but she wasn't quite ready to believe in something like that.

"So what caused you to study Tantra?" she asked.

"I've always been interested in energy and healing. I started meditating as a teenager and I learned to quiet my mind and listen to my own intuition. Once you do that, things come to you."

"So you learned about Tantra because some voice inside told you to?"

"I listen to my own knowing," he said. "I believe everyone knows what they need and can manifest it."

He sounded a lot like her sister. She talked about being guided by her higher self, while others talked about channeling spirits or angels, or all manner of energy beings. Hanna had always preferred her sister's description of knowing what you need for yourself rather than other random beings telling you what to do.

"It's just a matter of belief and authentic desire," he continued.

She wiggled and squeezed his cock again. "Well, I really desire an orgasm."

He stared straight into her eyes and said somberly, "Yes, but you don't believe you can have one."

She paused, dumbfounded. What had been a cute quip

suddenly became a deep insight. Hanna had seen the movie about visualizing what you want and making it real. Her sister had brought it over one day and sat Hanna down in front of the TV, adamant she watch it. Grey, too, poor guy. He never did know quite how to take Grace, though he was always gracious and accepting of her quirky ideas.

"I don't believe it?"

He kissed her forehead tenderly. "Not yet. But you will."

She stared at him, wide-eyed. She believed him. In fact, for the first time, she almost believed . . . maybe she really could . . .

She squeezed his delicious cock inside her, then tried to shift her hips away, but his hands remained firm on her back, not allowing her an inch. Unrelenting, she wiggled her hips sideways, to and fro, causing his solid cock to caress her soft vagina. A deep, thrumming pleasure pulsed through her. She squeezed and wiggled again. He remained completely motionless.

Remembering last night, she breathed deeply, thinking of the air as energy flowing through her body. She imagined her sacral chakra filling with this energy.

Waves of pleasure washed through her, and her breathing accelerated. She pushed her breasts hard against his chest and squeezed again, then moaned softly as a rising swell of pleasure cascaded through her, carrying her higher and higher. It was happening . . . she was sure of it. A heat like nothing she'd ever felt before burned through her and she . . .

Oh, my God. Panic lanced through her and she stopped cold, gasping for breath. She squeezed her vaginal muscles again, but this time to stop the flood of ferociously potent sensations. Frozen, afraid to move, she waited while the physical turmoil inside her slowly diminished.

Oh, God, she had come. Or . . . almost come. Maybe.

Hanna waved good-bye to J.M. as he drove down the street; then she turned to her front door and unlocked it. She was still a little stunned by what had happened only an hour ago in J.M.'s bed.

She stepped inside and jumped as she heard a murmur, like a soft snore. A blanket trailed over the back of her couch. She froze.

Had Grey shown up last night and let himself in? He still had a key. She'd let him store his stuff here until the end of his contract in New York, when he could set himself up in a new place. Still, it wasn't like him to come in uninvited.

Last night, after the class, he had told her he wasn't returning to New York right away. He'd said he'd call her so they could get together and talk.

Had he expected to stay here last night? But wouldn't he have said something then?

She slipped off her shoes and crept into the living room.

Unless maybe he'd been worried about her. Had he called her last night and fretted when he couldn't get ahold of her? The thought pleased her at the same time as it distressed her.

She peered around the couch at the blanket . . . and the face of her sister.

"Grace?"

Grace's eyelids fluttered open.

"Huh?" She blinked a few times, then focused on Hanna. "Oh, there you are."

"What do you mean, 'there you are'? What are you doing—?" Her hand clamped to her mouth as she remembered today was their day to go running together. "Oh, I'm so sorry. I totally forgot."

Poor Grace found it hard enough to get up at dawn without showing up here to find no running partner.

Grace pushed aside the blanket and sat up, a smile curling her lips.

"That's okay, sweetie." She patted the couch beside her. "Just sit down and tell me all about it."

"All about what?" Hanna sat down beside her big sister.

"About the man you spent the night with."

"I'd like to hear about that, too."

Hanna glanced toward the entrance and saw Grey closing the door behind him.

"What are you doing here?" Hanna rose to her feet, feeling a flush of heat staining her cheeks.

"I called you several times last night, until well after midnight. I got worried."

"I told you I was meeting someone."

He stepped into the room, his sour disposition apparent in the grim set of his jaw. His gaze flickered over her clothes—the same ones she'd been wearing last night when she'd talked to him after the class.

"I didn't think you'd spend the night with him."

Grace's gaze bounced from Hanna to Grey like someone watching a Ping-Pong match.

Hanna rubbed her arms, feeling suddenly cold. Past the steel hardness in his eyes, she could see the pain. She turned away, pacing across the room.

"Grey, we broke up two months ago. We're allowed to see other people."

She could feel his presence behind her, close. She could sense that he wanted to touch her, to cup her shoulders and draw her back against him. To break through the shield she'd placed against him. A shield in a sorry state of collapse, faced with his familiar, masculine presence.

She missed his tenderness. She missed the way he knew her better than anyone else—except Grace. They used to talk long into the night, about anything and everything. And they'd laughed so much together.

He could always sense when she was upset about something. He used to bring her peppermint tea and have her snuggle up beside him to talk about whatever was bothering her. She remembered the time she'd fretted about having to fire an employee and Grey had spent half the night talking it through with her, even though he'd had an early meeting the next morning.

He'd always made her feel cared for—and loved, even if he had never said the words. She missed that—and she missed him.

She couldn't lie to herself that she didn't love him. That her body didn't still crave him. Her skin quivered with the expectation of his touch. She could just turn around and step into his arms. Experience his strong, passionate lips against hers once again. She yearned to give herself over to his loving care, but a part of her, the stronger and more logical part, knew it was not to be. He might care about her, might even have convinced himself he wanted to keep her in his life, but he didn't love her.

"I know." His murmured words, so close behind her, sent a wave of melancholy through her. "I just wish you didn't want to."

She turned around and stared at him. He stood close, within arm's reach. Too close. Her heart thudded in her chest. To feel his arms around her again would be heaven.

But she wouldn't settle.

As much as she wanted to believe he actually did love her, that he just hadn't expressed it, she knew it didn't really matter. Even if he did love her, the fact that he wouldn't say it meant there was a problem. She needed to hear it, without having to ask. She needed a man who loved her so much, he would be bursting with the need to tell her. Not one who hid it inside, unable to express it.

Hanna concentrated on breathing as they stood there, a chasm of tumultuous emotions seething between them.

"Grey, I thought you were in New York," Grace said, breaking the oppressive silence.

He glanced at Grace. "That's right. I'm there on a contract for six months, but Hanna and I had decided to take a course together and I'm shifting my weekends to Wednesday and Thursday so I can drive back once a week to take it."

"Why were you calling?" Hanna asked.

His gaze met hers and the disappointment in his eyes unsettled her.

"You said you were calling me last night," she prompted. "Why?"

"I told you last night, I would like to talk to you."

She glanced at her watch. It was 8:15 and she still had to change and grab something to eat before she headed to the café for 9:30. She didn't even have time to squeeze in a run with Grace.

"I don't mean now," he said. "I'm on my way to a meeting myself. Since I couldn't get you on the phone I thought I'd stop by and see if I could catch you before you went to work so we could arrange something for later."

Hanna glanced toward Grace, who steadfastly stared out the back window toward the large oak tree with leaves fluttering in the light morning breeze.

Hanna nodded. "Okay, I could meet with you after work."

"Five, then?" he asked.

She hesitated, wondering if she should suggest after dinner, but then he'd probably suggest coming back here, or to wherever he was staying. In an intimate setting like that, given the strong feelings she still had for him, that could lead all too easily to another kind of intimacy. That wouldn't be fair to him, and it wouldn't be fair to J.M.

"I'll stop by and pick you up."

She nodded.

He glanced from her to Grace, then nodded too and said good-bye. As the door closed behind him, Hanna sank onto the couch beside Grace again.

Grace slid her arm around Hanna. "You're still in love with him, aren't you?"

"Give it up, Grace. I broke up with him two months ago."

"Okay, so tell me about this new guy. Did it work with him?"

Hanna flushed as she thought about earlier that morning.

"Well, I . . ." She glanced down at her hands, folded in her lap. "I'm not really sure."

Grace's forehead furrowed. "How can you not be sure?"

"I don't know." She felt in a daze as she remembered the sweeping wave of pleasure she'd felt with J.M. this morning. "It was different than I'd ever experienced. Like being swept away."

Grace took her hand and stared into Hanna's eyes with that deep concentration that always unsettled Hanna. As though Grace stared into her soul.

"Hanna, what are you afraid of?"

SIX

Grey sat in Dr. Jeremy Smith's guest chair facing his desk and waited silently while Jeremy—he'd told the class to call him by his first name—tapped his fingers on the wooden surface. A steady stream of students passed by the office, visible as hazy shapes through the frosted window in the wooden door as they headed to their next classes. Grey had plenty of time to talk, however, since Jeremy had set aside the whole hour. Apparently, not many students requested appointments at this time during summer semester.

Grey had told Jeremy about Hanna and how they'd been dating for over a year, how she couldn't come to climax, and that he wanted to find a way to help her.

He didn't mention she'd broken up with him two months ago. He didn't want the guy to think he was some kind of stalker.

Grey would do whatever it took to win Hanna back. Living without her was pure hell.

"Have you told her you love her?" Jeremy asked.

Shit.

The instructor's dark eyes bored straight into him, as if he could read all Grey's secrets.

"So you haven't."

"I'm sure that isn't the reason she can't . . ." His hands clenched under the table. "She never has before and . . . I just don't think it's related to me telling her how I feel about her."

Jeremy folded his hands on the desk and leaned forward. "You're right."

Grey just stared at him and blinked. Why the hell was the guy bringing it up if it didn't matter?

"A woman's partner has little to do with whether she achieves orgasm or not."

Grey's eyebrows rose. He'd like to think he had something to do with it. At least, with all the previous women he had been able to satisfy, and with great enthusiasm on their part. It was only Hanna he hadn't been able to take to that state of bliss.

"The responsibility lies with the woman herself," Jeremy continued. "The only way a woman can have an orgasm is if she can release herself to the pleasure of her body. You can help her do that."

"How?"

"You need to build up trust between you—"

"She trusts me."

"I'm sure she does, but I mean an intimate trust where she can be vulnerable to you. It would help if you told her you love her, so she knows you're not just going through the motions. Then she might be willing to open up, to drop her barriers when you're making love."

Grey's chest clenched. He wanted to tell her he loved her, and he would, then he would lay out all the facts and she'd have to make up her mind.

But to tell her now . . .

"You should also tell her how much you love being with her, how much you love giving her pleasure. This will help keep her focused on making love and the pleasure you're giving her rather than her fears and doubts about what you might be feeling about her."

Grey nodded. That part wouldn't be hard. He did love being with her, touching her, making love to her.

"Part of what you're doing is letting her know you aren't judging her for enjoying sex. That you don't consider her a bad girl."

"Why would she think that?"

J.M. watched the man sitting across from him. The guy obviously loved his woman. It shone in his eyes when he talked about her, and J.M. could sense it in Grey's energy.

"Even with today's more liberated attitudes about sex, there is still a perception that a woman who enjoys sex too much may be considered morally questionable, even if only in her own mind. That's why you want to reassure her that you love making love to her, that you find her sexy and exciting, that giving her pleasure gives you pleasure.

"I have some books I can recommend." J.M. slid two across his desk. "And a couple I can lend you."

Grey picked up the books J.M. pushed in front of him. "But these are about hypnosis."

"That's right. The things I've suggested today are from Tantric teachings and they'll help, but to learn some of the stronger Tantric techniques, like breathing and drawing sexual energy through your bodies, will take more time and training.

"In the meantime, you can use hypnosis to relax her," J.M. continued, "and to help get her past her barriers. The key is to be clear about what you will do in a session, and to stick with it."

Grey lifted one book and scanned the back jacket. "It looks like this one is for hypnotizing someone to live out a fantasy."

"Fantasies are a great way to set free our inner desires, by putting them in a framework we can access. Read the book and see what appeals to you and what you'd like to try. We can get together again next week and discuss it so you can proceed with your first session with your girl-friend."

Grey stared at him quizzically. "You think I can read one book and hypnotize her in a week?"

"The hardest part is the induction—taking her into the trance. Those skilled at hypnosis can easily use their voice to relax their subjects and draw them into a hypnotic state. I have some tapes of relaxing music. You can use them to establish that state. Then you can use some of the scripts in that book—modified to your own needs—to take her through a session."

Grey opened his backpack and tucked the books inside.

"Okay, I'll see you next week." He stood up and offered his hand. They clasped hands, and J.M. shook warmly.

"Thank you for your help," Grey said.

The heartfelt words filled J.M. with a warm, peaceful energy. *This is what it's all about. Helping people.* He knew his books helped people, but that was so distant. Actually working with someone one-on-one made J.M. feel great, especially when the guy so clearly loved his girlfriend.

J.M. smiled as he watched Grey head out the office door. She was a lucky woman, because J.M. could tell Grey would do whatever it took to keep her.

J.M. opened the door to the Hot Spot Café and stepped inside. He joined the end of the line where several customers waited for service. Hanna stuffed a large muffin into a bag, then handed it, along with a tall cup, to an elderly woman with glasses, while the young woman beside Hanna handed three cups to a young denim-clad man with a backpack.

After a few moments in line, J.M. was next to be served. The woman in front of him moved aside, and Hanna glanced up. Her eyes glittered as her lips turned up in a smile when she saw him.

He leaned toward her and murmured, "Do you think your boss would let you take a break? I have something I want to talk to you about."

The clerk beside Hanna, who had watched the exchange carefully, laughed. "She *is* the boss. Hanna owns the place."

"Really?" He noticed a slight flush to Hanna's cheeks. Was she embarrassed at her success? He quirked his eyebrows up. "So?"

Hanna glanced at the three people behind J.M. "Well, I—"

"No worries, Hanna. I can handle the line."

Hanna nodded, then turned away and prepared a couple of teas. She walked around the counter and he followed her. When he placed his hand on the small of her back, she quickened her pace, as if to keep out of his reach.

She led him to a table in the back corner, away from the windows, thus away from the busiest tables. In fact, it was their table—where they had made love. She must have remembered that, too, because her cheeks flushed a rosy, and quite becoming, shade of pink.

He peeled the lid off his tea and took a sip. Just the right amount of milk and sugar. She knew what he liked. He reached out to take her hand, but she slipped it under the table, out of reach.

"Is there something wrong?"

"No, why do you ask?"

"You don't want me to hold your hand?"

Most women loved such shows of affection, but he sensed that right now she would not welcome anything that showed they were a couple.

She didn't deny it, just sipped her tea.

"Don't you want people to know we're together?" An uneasiness settled into him. "Or am I assuming too much?"

"No, of course not. I wouldn't have slept with you if . . ." She glanced at the love seat where she'd kissed him, then stripped off her blouse and thrust her naked breasts at him. She blushed an even brighter red. "I mean—"

He grinned. "Yes, I know what you mean." He watched her, waiting for her answer.

She shifted in her chair. "It's just that . . . People here are used to seeing me with my ex-boyfriend and . . ."

He frowned. "You did say your *ex*-boyfriend, right? You aren't still seeing him?"

"No, of course not. He's in New York. Except . . .

Well, he did come into town yesterday and he wants to talk to me."

J.M. knew this shouldn't bother him at all, but strange, possessive feelings tightened his gut. He wanted to ask why the guy wanted to talk to her, wanted to find out if he was going to try to win her back, but resisted. J.M. wouldn't be one of those jealous jerks. Either this relationship would move forward or it wouldn't, as it was meant to do.

He laid his hand on the table in open invitation, wanting to touch her, hoping she would slip her hand into his.

Hanna stared at his big, masculine hand lying on the table and her fingers itched to reach out and touch him. She remembered what pleasure that hand had given her, last night and before . . . right on this chair.

What was wrong with her? The man was absolutely gorgeous. Any woman would be thrilled to hold hands with him in public, showing her claim to him. But Hanna was afraid her staff would think less of her or her customers would think her actions inappropriate if she sat at a table mooning over a guy.

"You don't have to worry about what they think, you know?"

She glanced at him sharply. How did he know what she was thinking?

Sometimes Grace did that and claimed it was intuition, or being in tune with the universal consciousness, or just the ability to read people. Grace used the different explanations interchangeably, saying people could accept whichever one fit their own belief system best.

Hanna just thought it was spooky. Now J.M. was doing it.

But he was right. She realized she let her worries about what other people thought influence her far too much.

She liked J.M . . . she was dating him . . . there was no reason she couldn't hold his hand in public, even at her place of work. It was a café, for heaven's sake, not a business office.

Could her worry about what people thought of her be part of the fear of orgasm that Grace had postulated this morning? When Grace had made the comment, Hanna had rejected it. After all, she couldn't think of any reason why she would be afraid of having an orgasm. But now she wondered . . . was she afraid of what her lover might think of her, allowing herself such wanton, uninhibited pleasure? The thought of quivering in orgasm made her feel vulnerable.

But she felt sure J.M. wouldn't judge her.

She slipped her hand into his and instantly felt a thrill of awareness careen through her. Oh, man, she would love to slip into his arms and kiss him silly. She shifted in her chair as she remembered what else she had done with him at her place of work.

He squeezed her hand gently and his smile melted through her.

The bell over the door tinkled and Hanna automatically glanced toward the entrance.

Grey?

seven

Hanna's hand jerked away from J.M.'s as she watched the tall man with sandy brown hair and a black jacket step inside. Her heart nearly stopped.

But no, the man bore only a superficial resemblance to Grey.

She glanced at the clock and realized that Grey had said he'd arrive in about half an hour, but knowing him, he might show up any time now.

She had to get J.M. out of here. She did not want to find herself in the awkward position of having both men in the same place at the same time. Sizing each other up.

She sucked down a third of her tea, which had cooled substantially.

"I need to get back to work. I have some paperwork to get done before I leave, and I'm meeting my friend after work." She eased her chair back, then paused. "Oh, you had something you wanted to talk to me about?"

"I just wanted to tell you how amazing last night was. And ask you out on Friday. Dinner at my place?"

She smiled. "I'd love to."

"Ready to go?" Grey stood in the doorway to her office.

"Almost." Hanna keyed the last stock receipt total into the worksheet, watched the sum increment, then saved and closed the spreadsheet package. She clicked SHUT DOWN, then closed the laptop computer and straightened up the papers on her desk.

"Okay, all set." She strode toward the door and followed Grey from her quiet office.

The bell over the outside door chimed as another customer entered the shop, then joined the lineup at the counter. Four people stood in line, but Sandy was handling the customers with her usual quick but friendly efficiency. The current customer laughed at something Sandy said, then picked up his cup and stepped away from the counter. Sandy smiled at the next man in line.

"Sandy, I'm on my way," Hanna said as soon as he'd finished ordering. "Jessica will be in at seven to help out with the rush."

There was a concert over at Radford Hall tonight, so Hanna had brought in an extra staff member to handle the crowd that would inevitably collect in the coffee shop before the concert. It was a good thing she had students who were happy to work a couple of hours at a time to pick up extra pocket money.

"Okay. See you tomorrow." Sandy smiled widely at Grey. "It was great seeing you again, Grey."

Hanna gritted her teeth. She knew Sandy probably thought Grey's arrival was a sign that he and Hanna would reconcile. Sandy was a sweet kid and she believed in storybook endings. Now Hanna would feel awkward whenever J.M. showed up in the shop, worried that Sandy would think she was cheating on Grey. Not that she should care what Sandy thought.

Grey held the door open for Hanna and she stepped outside into the bright summer afternoon.

"The car's around the corner," Grey said, and she followed him along the sidewalk.

Forester Street was busy this time of day. Nothing like the big city, of course, which was why Hanna liked living in this quiet university town alongside the picturesque river.

The delicate scent of roses wafted from the garden in front of the redbrick house beside the ice-cream shop next to the Hot Spot Café, and the strains of classical guitar drifted from the music shop across the narrow side street as she and Grey turned the corner. His silver Corvette, sleek and shiny, sat by the second parking meter.

A large truck whooshed by and its horn blared at a small blue Echo darting in front of it. Hanna glanced around at the sudden noise and the tip of her shoe caught on a crack in the sidewalk and she lurched forward, straight into Grey. His arms came around her, preventing her fall but sending her reeling against his chest. Warmth seeped through her at the feel of his body against hers. Her gaze locked with his and she knew.

He was going to kiss her.

Grey stared at Hanna's sweet, angelic face. Her soft body pressed against his was too much for him.

He tightened his arms around her and captured her lips. The stunning feel of her soft mouth under his took his breath away.

Hanna's brain demanded she pull away, but the rest of her melted into the kiss like ice cream on a hot summer sidewalk. His mouth, sexy and full, coaxed hers with gentle movement, then his tongue stroked the seam of her lips. She opened like a flower to sunlight, desperate for his tender invasion. And totally stunned at his unprecedented show of affection in public.

She could barely catch her breath as his tongue stroked inside her mouth, his lips moving softly on hers. She sighed, then mustered all her strength to draw away slowly, missing him more with every inch of distance between them. His eyes filled with longing as he watched her withdraw.

"I'm sorry."

That's all he said. Then he tucked his arm around her waist and guided her to the car, then opened the door for her.

Ten minutes later, he pulled onto Kent Street, then parked in front of Leone's, a wonderful Italian restaurant.

"I know you like their chicken Marsala."

She nodded, then accompanied him inside.

"What's this all about?" she asked, once they'd settled into the restaurant and the waiter had taken their order.

She grabbed a warm roll from the basket the waiter had dropped off at their table, broke it open, and buttered it, the yeasty aroma making her mouth water.

"Hanna, there's something important I have to tell you. I was wrong—"

She put down her butter knife. "Grey, it's over between us. I'm already seeing someone else. I don't mean to hurt you, but you should know that we've already spent the night together. And I really like him."

Grey remained outwardly calm, but she noticed the flicker of emotion in his eyes. A few moments passed before he responded. "All right, I accept that. But we're still friends and I care about your happiness. Can I still be a part of your life, Hanna?"

"Yes, we can still be friends, but that's all we can be to each other. No more."

"Then I'm sure it's fine if I tell you that I've decided to keep taking the Kama Sutra class we signed up for. I know you're not happy about your bedroom issues, and I still want to find out how to help you."

"Grey, I said just friends. I don't think practicing Kama Sutra positions together would be appropriate."

"Hear me out. I'm not suggesting you hop into bed with me again, though obviously I'd love that." He grinned wickedly.

Her eyebrows arched upward. "Then what are you suggesting?"

"I've been talking to the instructor about you."

"Oh, no." She rested her face in her hands. Images of Grey chatting to the class about her problem spiraled through her head.

"He's agreed to meet with me on Wednesday mornings after the course to kick around ideas to help with this."

She sucked in a breath and faced him again.

"Why would he want to help me when I'm not in his class?"

"I told him you're my girlfriend."

She stroked her finger around the rim of her water glass.

"You mean *ex*-girlfriend." But she didn't scold him for lying to his instructor. It wasn't her place. And anyway, she couldn't help thinking it was kind of sweet of Grey. At the same time, she worried that he must be holding out hopes that maybe he could win her back. She should stomp those hopes into the ground, but as she stared at his handsome, familiar face, she realized she wasn't willing to let go of him yet. She still held out a hope that maybe they would get back together again.

But where would that leave J.M.?

"And how would you achieve this feat without me hopping in bed with you?"

"The instructor has suggested some techniques—"

Hanna choked on the water she'd been sipping, imagining Grey armed with the Kama Sutra and various sexual techniques laying her down on a bed and triggering an eruption of bliss.

"Techniques to help you understand what might be blocking you and why. For instance, today he suggested we try hypnosis."

"You mean, go to a hypnotherapist?"

"He actually suggested we do a session where I act as the hypnotist."

She stared at him dubiously. Did he think he could use a hypnotic suggestion to change her mind about being with him? But that didn't sound like Grey. He wouldn't want to trick her into being with him.

"He recommended some books and suggested I use background music to help guide you into a hypnotic trance to find out what kind of fantasies might increase your sexual excitement."

Fantasies? A nuzzling heat pushed through her. Experiencing sexual fantasies with Grey was a very exciting thought.

But totally inappropriate.

"I assumed you'd say something about lowering my inhibitions." So she could relax.

"I didn't think you'd be comfortable with that, but as part of seeking your fantasies we would lower your barriers a little. Just enough to allow you to express yourself freely."

"But why you? Why not a trained hypnotherapist?"

"The idea is you'd be in a relaxed setting with someone you trust." He gazed at her frankly. "What do you say? Would you give me a chance to see where this might go?"

"I don't think that would be fair to the other man I'm seeing."

Grey leaned forward and clasped her hands. "Tell me one thing. You spent the night with him last night. Did it work any better with him?"

Her eyebrows drew together and her brow furrowed. He nodded, clearly drawing the conclusion that it hadn't.

"Okay, so do you want to continue never knowing that joy or do you want to work with me and take a chance at experiencing something you've only dreamed of?"

She hesitated. She longed to experience an orgasm and Grey was offering something substantial to try. But by having sex with J.M. she'd already committed to him on some level. And from her experience this morning, she felt it was just a matter of time before she found the big O in his arms.

"All I'm asking right now is that you meet with me next week and try the hypnosis. See where it goes. All we'll do is talk during the session, nothing more. Find out what might help you. Before we start, we'll fully discuss what is going to happen while you're in the trance."

He squeezed her hands.

"Hanna, don't you owe it to yourself to give this a shot?"

She shook her head. "I don't know."

"All you're agreeing to is meeting with me next week and doing one hypnosis session. That's all."

"Where we talk? Nothing more?"

"Exactly. After we see how that goes, then you can decide if you'll see me the following week to do more hypnosis work."

She pursed her lips. What kind of fool was she to even consider this?

But Grey's proposition intrigued her. As long as she could convince him there would be nothing sexual between them, what was the harm?

Despite the fact that he would be hypnotizing her to find her block against sexual climax. To find out what her sexual fantasies were.

She had to admit, the thought of finding out her inner fantasies excited her. She couldn't imagine doing it with anyone else. Grey knew her. Intimately. She felt safe with him. He was probably the only person in the world that she could do this with.

"Okay."

Instantly upon agreeing, she felt selfish, as if she was taking advantage of him, but at the beaming smile he gave her, she couldn't bear to withdraw her permission.

eight

As Hanna approached J.M.'s front door, excitement quivered through her. It had been two days since she'd talked with Grey. The same day she'd almost lost herself in J.M.'s arms. Between the effervescent, vivid excitement of being with someone new and the deep, emotional feelings triggered by her encounter with Grey, she'd been riding an emotional wave all week. Her dreams were filled with the two handsome men and *lots* of sex.

She woke up hungry and wanting. Right now, knowing J.M. stood on the other side of this door sent her hormones whirling into a maelstrom.

She pressed the doorbell. A gentle chime sounded.

A few seconds passed, then the antique brass doorknob turned and the door pulled open.

"Hi there." J.M. smiled, revealing straight white teeth.

He looked absolutely fabulous, wearing a long-sleeved black shirt in a soft-looking fabric, the top few buttons open. Her gaze rested on the small triangle of muscular chest, setting her heart thumping. His jeans—in black as usual— accentuated his long legs and narrow waist.

Her gaze returned to his face. His square jaw. His well-sculpted cheekbones. His warm, inviting brown eyes.

She smiled, hoping she didn't look too ridiculous as she stared at him with longing.

"Hi."

He stepped back to let her inside, then closed the door behind her. She slipped off her sandals, then stepped to-ward him. He drew her into his arms and pulled her close, his lips meeting hers with a hunger that matched her own.

Oh, God, his hard, muscular body felt so good. His strong arms around her. His lips caressing hers. His tongue slipped between her lips as she stroked it with her own, loving the instant intimacy between them. Her breathing accelerated and she wanted to tear off her clothes. Right after she tore off his.

His arms stroked her back and the kiss heated up. Her breasts pressed hard into his chest, the nipples beading to incredible tightness. Her sex tightened and pulsed. She wanted to wrap her legs around him, ready for his hot, hard erection to spear into her. She could feel it growing against her belly.

At this rate, the dinner he'd promised to cook for her would be left uneaten in the kitchen, at least for a few hours.

She drew back and smiled up at him. He took her hand and led her to the couch, then they both sat down beside each other. A large platter of veggies and dip sat in the middle of the square coffee table, along with bowls of nuts, a platter of cheese, and a plate of fancy crackers. She grabbed a stick of celery, dipped it, then took a bite.

"Mmm. Delicious."

"So how did your conversation go with your ex-boyfriend the other day?" he asked.

Darn. She'd hoped he wouldn't remember that.

"Fine."

She took a piece of broccoli and munched on it. She didn't want to tell J.M. about Grey's suggestion to do the hypnosis. J.M. probably wouldn't understand—she didn't really understand it herself—and he would probably make more of it than it was.

She stroked the back of his hand, then turned it over and raised it to her lips. She kissed his palm, loving the feel of his big, strong hand against her mouth. His other hand stroked along her cheek, then cupped her head and drew her face to his. He kissed her, sweet and loving, then hugged her close.

Over his shoulder, she noticed several pictures on the fireplace mantel.

"Is that your family?" she asked.

He glanced toward the fireplace.

"Yes, my mother and father," he pointed to the large photo frame in the center, "and my two sisters to the right, and that's my brother and his wife and two sons on the left."

"And all the gorgeous young women?" She smiled and nodded toward the five photos of very pretty young ladies ranging in age from about sixteen to midtwenties arranged neatly on one of the bookshelves across from the couch.

"Those are my nieces. The three on the left are Simone's—that's my oldest sister—Susan, Claire, and Diana. The two on the right are Regina's—and they are Chantal and Ellen."

"They are lovely. Where do they live?"

"Well, Simone and her husband moved to Australia five years ago and both Regina and Roger still live in Colorado. That's where we grew up. Mom and Dad are there, too."

"It must be hard being so far away from your family. I guess you don't see them a lot."

"Mostly just at Christmastime—and I haven't seen Simone since she moved out of the country. We all keep in touch by phone, though. And e-mail."

She nodded. She couldn't imagine being that far away from Grace. Especially since their parents died a couple of years ago.

"I'm lucky my sister lives in town," she said.

"What are your parents like?"

"They are . . . were . . . very old-fashioned."

"I take it they had old-fashioned values, too?"

At her use of the past tense, she'd seen in his eyes that he'd understood that her parents were gone, but she liked the fact that he didn't dwell on it. He just allowed her to talk about them, without hampering the moment by commenting on their passing.

"Oh, yeah. My sister and I weren't allowed to date until we were eighteen, and it was made very clear to us that a young woman didn't engage in sexual activity until after she was married. And even then, she wasn't supposed to enjoy it." She laughed, but his eyebrows arched upward. "Oh, you think that's why . . ." She shook her head. "They didn't really say that. My sister and I just used to kid each other about that."

"You do realize their attitude might have something to do with your inability to orgasm, though."

"I suppose, but my sister doesn't have any problems. Or so she tells me."

"Different people react differently to the same stimuli. You might have been more concerned with pleasing them than your sister was."

"Well, that's true. My sister has always been her own person. She took a lot of flack from Mom and Dad when she got divorced, but she took it in stride. She always made it clear to them that she loved them, but that she'd live her own life."

"I'd love to meet this sister of yours."

"She'd love that, too. She likes to keep tabs on the men I'm dating."

"She's your older sister, I take it."

"That's right. And I have a feeling the two of you would get along famously. And I have a feeling she'd think you're very good for me."

"Oh, yeah?" He moved a little closer. "And why is that?"

"Well, she would love the fact you're taking that Kama Sutra course, for one. She'll figure you can help me with my *problem*. In fact, if she could have set me up with the instructor, she would have."

Hanna grabbed a carrot from the platter and bit off the end.

He cleared his throat and his gaze captured hers in an unsettling manner. "And what about you? Would you like to go out with the instructor?"

Her stomach clenched at the thought.

"Hell, no. If that instructor walked in here right now, I'd hightail it out of here." She pointed the partially munched carrot stick at him to emphasize her words. "I don't want to be around anyone who's *that* comfortable with sex." She waved the carrot back and forth. "Sacred sex. Energy sex. Whole-body orgasms."

"I take it you've been reading the course material."

"The guy just seems like some kind of spiritual master, but for sex. I'd feel way too lame around him."

She watched J.M. as she popped the rest of the carrot in her mouth, chewed, and swallowed it. His proximity, the heat emanating from his body, the simmering sensuality in his eyes kicked her hormones into high gear. She leaned toward him and wrapped her hands around his neck.

"Now you . . . you know more than the average guy. You've studied some interesting stuff . . . but you're not intimidating." She leaned forward and nuzzled his ear. "In fact, I find you very . . ." She nipped his earlobe. ". . . very . . ." She nuzzled his jawline, below his ear. ". . . easy to be around."

"So do you think your sister would be right . . . that I can help you with your problem?" He stroked her hair and smiled warmly.

His proximity, the heat emanating from his body, the simmering sensuality in his eyes kicked her hormones into high gear.

She smiled. "Well, yes, I think maybe you can."

He tucked his finger under her chin and kissed her. His lips moved tenderly on hers, and heat blossomed through her. Her arms curled tighter around his neck and she drew him closer, her tongue delving between his lips. His strength surrounded her. His tenderness melted her and made her feel faint with need.

Her lips parted from his and she sucked in a breath, then nuzzled the base of his neck. She kissed downward, following the opening of his shirt, then released his buttons one by one.

She grasped his belt buckle, drawing in slow, deep breaths, and pulled it open, then released the top button. She ran her hand over the denim-encased bulge in front of her, longing to release it and draw it into her mouth, but when she reached for the zipper he covered her hand with his and drew it to his mouth, then pressed his lips to her palm.

"Slow down, sweetheart. We've got all night."

He drew her to her feet and led her to the kitchen.

For the first time, she noticed the wonderful aroma of spices filling the house. On the sleek black marble countertop he had several trays of exotic foods. Small chunks of meat in delectable sauces, vegetables, dips, and fruit.

"Are you hungry?" he asked.

She turned to him, not even trying to hide her desire to devour him.

"Starving." She curled her arms around him and melted against him. Her lips fused with his in a passionate, heart–melting kiss.

His arms tightened around her and she felt herself being lifted. She felt cold, smooth marble on the backs of her legs as he set her on the counter, their lips still locked in the searing kiss.

When their lips parted, he smiled at her.

"I'm glad you brought your appetite."

He lifted a dark chunk of meat and grazed it across her lips, then held it. She opened her mouth and he eased the meat inside. A savory tang burst across her tongue. She captured his fingers inside her mouth, licking and sucking them until he withdrew. Slowly. She chewed the delicious morsel and swallowed, increasing her hunger for food to almost rival her hunger for J.M.

He fed her another chunk of meat, followed by a cube of papaya.

He stood pressed against the counter, facing her, their eyes level. She could feel his muscular torso against her inner thighs, the heat of him pushing close to her intimate opening.

She didn't know how much more of this she could take.

She grabbed a piece of meat and fed it to him. The feel of his tongue encircling her finger and thumb as he drew them into his warm, moist mouth thrilled her senses.

He fed her a piece of tangy, sweet pineapple and kissed her throat as she chewed and swallowed. His lips nuzzled the base of her neck, in the curve of her collarbone, while his hands stroked up and down her sides. She drew her T-shirt over her head, then tossed it aside, revealing her low-cut lacy black and red bra.

He trailed the tip of his tongue over one breast, following the line of the lacy cup, then over the other. She wanted him to tug the bra down and feast on her aching nipples, but instead he plucked another piece of meat from the tray and fed it to her, followed by a chunk of celery in a heavenly sesame dressing.

She glanced to the trays and selected a juicy piece of chicken in a dark, aromatic sauce. She raised it to his lips and stroked under his lower lip, down to his chin, then into his mouth. She leaned forward and lapped her tongue over his chin, then up to his lip. She nibbled his lip into her mouth, savoring the spicy sauce, but more, the feel of his full lip captured between her lips. She licked it, then sucked. He rewarded her with a soft moan.

Her hands traveled over his broad shoulders, then over his biceps, drawing them around her. She slid forward, wrapping her legs around his back, pulling him closer. She arched her pelvis forward and sucked in a breath when his hard, ridged stomach came in contact with her hot, needy sex. She rocked against him, wishing their clothes would melt away so she could feel skin on skin.

He fed her a mushroom, then licked her lips. She sucked the tip of his tongue into her mouth. She reached for a big, fat blackberry and brushed his cheek with the nubby fruit. He eased back and she drew half into her mouth, leaving the other half exposed, then leaned forward. He grasped the fruit and drew it into his mouth. When their lips met, she swirled her tongue into his mouth, tasting the same tangy sweetness in his mouth as hers. The fruit dissolved and she swallowed, then plunged her tongue into his mouth again.

She grabbed a strawberry and crushed it in her hand, then smeared it along his neck and down his chest. She licked and nibbled her way downward. She grasped the opening of his shirt and pushed it wide open, then stroked the next strawberry across his chest, covering both nipples. She lapped across one side, circling the nipple without touching it, then lapped across the other side. With her fingertips, she circled a tasty blackberry over his nipple, then pinched the berry between her fingertips, squeezing his nipple. She pushed the fruit tight against his nipple with her tongue, pushing and cajoling him as she devoured it, then nibbling his nipple until he groaned in pleasure.

The same treatment on his other nipple had him crumbling to her will.

She hoped.

She stroked up and down his chest, then captured his lips with her fruit-smeared lips. He licked them clean, then lapped inside her mouth in search of more sweetness. She wrapped her arms around his neck and kissed him in earnest, feeling a depth of passion she'd never experienced before. She wanted to climb inside him. Become one with him.

She kissed down his throat and down his chest. His labored breathing encouraged her. She slipped from the counter and kissed down his belly, then tugged down his zipper. His cock pushed from the dark briefs as if seeking her presence. She licked him, right over the tip of his delicious penis, as she pulled the fly of his jeans apart, then tugged his briefs down. His cock sprang forward, spearing outward from his jeans. She pushed his jeans down, letting them fall to the floor with a thump of leather and heavy fabric on ceramic tile.

She licked him from base to tip, then began thoroughly licking the bulbous tip, her tongue exploring every curve and ridge. She swirled in circles under the swell of the corona, then lapped over the top and dipped the tip of her tongue tight against the tiny hole. The tart taste of precum greeted her.

She wrapped her lips around him, then glided her lips downward, until she'd swallowed all of his considerable length into her mouth. Then she pulled back. His hands grasped her shoulders and he drew her upward, then captured her lips in a delicious kiss. He lifted her back onto the counter and kissed her soundly.

"Have you had enough to eat?" he asked.

She rolled her eyes down to his delightful exposed cock and smiled.

"Not yet, but if you'd give me a minute."

He chuckled, then kissed her again. "I mean food, sweetheart."

"I think I've had enough for now."

He stepped out of his pants and kicked them aside, then reached across the counter for a green bottle chilling in an ice bucket.

"How about some champagne?"

"I'd love some."

He popped the cork and poured the bubbly amber liquid into two tall crystal flutes. He picked one up and held it to her lips. She sipped. The effervescent liquid danced along her throat. He sipped, then kissed her again.

She wrapped her legs around him, trapping his big cock between her thighs, the heat of him scorching through her clothes.

He picked her up and carried her through the door. He settled her on the couch, then turned back to the kitchen, returning a moment later with the two glasses of wine and the ice bucket with the bottle.

She stood up and opened her jeans, then dropped them to the floor. She stood before him in her sexy lace bra and a matching red and black lace thong. She turned around and leaned over to pick up her jeans, purposely giving him an eyeful of her nearly naked behind.

"My God, you are sexy."

He stepped behind her and pulled her close to his body. She could feel his hot, hard rod pressing against her buttocks. She rocked her pelvis against him.

"Mmm." He turned her in his arms and kissed her. "You've tasted me—now it's my turn to taste you."

At his sexy smile, her breath caught. Oh, God, she wanted him. She pulled the cups of her bra under her breasts, delighted by the dark simmering of his gaze as she exposed the naked mounds. He eased her onto the couch and spread her thighs, then knelt before her. He lifted his glass and took a sip, then leaned toward her breast. She gasped as he sucked her nipple into his mouth—into cold, bubbly champagne. It thrust sharply into his mouth as it swelled. The liquid warmed as he sucked on her. His tongue laved over her nipple. He released it and took another sip, then treated her other nipple to the same torment.

She leaned back against the pillows and enjoyed his suckling, her eyes drifting closed. His hot mouth warmed both nipples as he continued to nibble and suck. One. Then the other. Back and forth.

Her eyelids snapped open as cold liquid splashed across her chest and down her stomach, dribbling onto her panties. He smiled as he put the bottle down on the table and proceeded to lick her skin clean. He slipped his fingers under the band of her thong and slid it down her legs, then tossed it aside. He lifted her legs and placed her heels on the coffee table behind him, then grabbed the bottle again and winked at her as he tipped the bottle up. A second later, cold liquid spilled over her folds.

"Ohhh!"

His mouth covered her and the cold turned to seething heat, bubbling through her entire body. His tongue lapped at her slit, then slipped inside her, licking the mouth of her vagina with careful scrutiny. He slipped two fingers inside and slid them in and out, then parted her flesh. When he reached for the bottle again, she knew exactly what he was going to do but still wasn't prepared for the shocking sensation of cold as the frigid liquid filled her opening. He slipped his tongue into her and lapped greedily, then licked her until all sensation of cold had been replaced with astonishing heat.

His tongue laved her sex, stroking the mouth with

long, hot strokes. His mouth covered her, and he sucked her rippled flesh into his mouth. His tongue dabbed at her clitoris and then he drew on it in gentle pulses, building, deeper and longer, until he sucked hard and fast. Heat began in waves, suffusing every part of her body, washing from her head to her toes and back again, but always centered around his wonderful, pleasure-giving mouth.

"Oh, yes. That is so . . . Ohhh."

She moaned as he licked and swirled his tongue around and around the tight bundle of nerves, then pressed with his tongue and she thought she would explode with pleasure.

Oh, God, was this an orgasm? Would she finally . . . ? Her body tensed and the blossoming pleasure receded. No, she couldn't let it get away. She tangled her hands in his hair, her fingertips dancing across his scalp as she drew him closer, but his tongue slowed and he drew back, then kissed up her belly.

Was he giving up?

If he was, could she really blame him? She was a losing proposition, after all.

She pushed forward and urged him onto the couch, then took a sip of champagne, then sucked his cock into her mouth, bathing him in cold. He groaned, then curled his fingers through her hair as she pulsed her head up and down, loving the feel of his hard shaft gliding through her mouth. She swallowed, then sucked him deep into her mouth, then pulsed some more. She settled on the head and spiraled around, licking under the ridge.

"Sweetheart, that is incredible, but you are not going to make me come. Not before I show you your first orgasm."

His hands grasped her shoulders and she felt herself tumbled backward and her legs spread wide. He smiled as he dove down to her pussy and began to lick and suck once again. To her total surprise, within seconds he had her gasping, almost at the same height as before. His tongue circled her clit, then he sucked and her pleasure spiked again. A sense of euphoria washed through her, but without the tension. Could it be that . . . ? The pleasure rose and she sighed, lying back and enjoying his ministrations. Her body started to quiver and she sucked in a deep breath. Heat crept along every nerve ending and she knew an orgasm was within reach. And she wanted it bad.

She rocked her pelvis forward and clung to his head, holding him close to her. His tongue worked busily, building the heat, filling her with pleasure.

She gasped as the target approached. Closer. And closer. Her muscles ached, stiffening as she readied herself. Maybe this time . . .

But he stopped, drawing away and smiling down at her. She groaned as she felt the heat wash away. She had been so close. Hadn't he realized?

"I almost . . ."

He lifted her onto the couch again and knelt in front of her.

"We're going to do better than almost."

His fingers slid inside her. Two. Then three. He stroked her insides, gliding over her slick inner flesh. It felt incredible. Her legs quivered. Her hand reached for his cock, clinging to its hot, hard length for stability. As he stroked, he leaned forward and licked her clit and she wailed at the unfathomable pleasure.

"Ohhhh, yes. Oh, my . . ."

Pleasure overwhelmed her. Her abdominal muscles tightened, and her sex contracted as she tried to grab the pleasure and pull it inside her. She wanted it so much. She had to have it.

Closer and closer. Never had she felt so much pleasure. She always thought when she'd passed the peak of pleasure she couldn't get it back, but J.M. had already brought her to a peak twice. Each time she'd lost it, he'd brought her back again.

Maybe this time.

She gasped as his fingers plunged deeper and he sucked her clit with patient determination.

Here it comes. Here it comes!

J.M. shifted, removing his mouth and hand, and she wailed at the interruption.

He scooped her into his arms and carried her into the bedroom. As he rested her on the bed, he murmured into her ear.

"Don't worry, darling. We can bring it back any time we want."

He knew. God damn it, he was doing it on purpose. Part of her was angry and wanted to scream at him. Another part of her demanded she let him have his way, understanding deep inside he knew exactly what she needed.

He sat her on the edge of the bed and plunked a cushion on the floor, then knelt on it. He spread her legs and slid his long, hard cock into her. She groaned at the exquisite pleasure of his hot hardness spearing into her.

"Oh, yes." She couldn't believe how intense the pleasure was. She was already close to that blissful state. He pushed deep, until he was fully immersed in her. But instead of moving inside her, he remained still. She closed her eyes and squeezed him, trying to draw him deeper inside. She didn't try to urge him to move, waiting to see what he would do. She felt his body shift, then heard a whirring sound.

He kissed her neck, then nuzzled behind her ear, sending the fine hairs along her neck dancing.

"Sweetheart," he murmured. He kissed her, moving his lips in a primal dance.

Something moved against her wrist and she glanced down to see a long red penis-shaped vibrator pulsing against the soft white flesh of her wrist.

"I'm going to use this."

He lifted it and brushed it against her lips. Without

thinking, she licked her lips and wrapped them around the red dildo. The soft, pulsing movement in her mouth excited her. He drew it from her mouth and licked it, then drew it into his own mouth. She licked the shaft as it pulsed in his mouth.

His hand covered her breast and squeezed as he trailed the damp red plastic penis down her chest. He eased her back until she lay on the bed, her legs draped over the edge. His cock, still embedded deep within her, twitched as the second penis nuzzled her clit. At the intense sensation, she wailed, sure she would go flying over the edge any second. Her muscles tensed, intensifying the feel of his hard cock within her.

"Oh, God." She felt like crying, the pleasure was so intense.

He pulled the red cock away and the pleasure withdrew—a little.

"I was sooo close."

"I know."

Damn him. He gave her so much pleasure.

He pushed the red penis to her clit again and instantly she was right back where she'd been.

"Oh, yes. Oh, God."

He pulsed and twirled the cock against her as his cock filled her with pleasure just by being inside her. Heat washed through her, and her body quivered helplessly. She lay still . . . waiting . . . wanting. . . . It was so close.

Rising heat. Intense delight. Deafening need.

"Yes . . . oh, yes. . . ." Her voice quivered helplessly. "Please. Yes. . . ."

So close.

He pulled the red penis away again and kissed her, pulling her into his arms. He shifted so that he sat on the bed and she straddled him, her knees on each side, his cock still inside her. He lifted her a little and she felt the vibrating red cock quiver against her ass, then nudge her opening.

"Ohhh. . . ."

It pushed inside a little, then withdrew. New sensation swirled through her, hot and intense. It pushed again, going a little deeper, then withdrew. His finger swept over her clit and she wailed, loud and needy.

The red cock pushed inside her as his finger quivered against her clit and she almost screamed at the intensity of the pleasure.

"Oh, God, I'm coming, I'm—"

He stood up, jarring her from the impending cataclysm.

"What are you doing?" she demanded.

He carried her into the living room and slid open the patio door. The warm night air caressed her heated skin. His penis still embedded deep inside her, he carried her into the moonlit yard. He walked down steps and she felt warm water caress her feet, then spill up her legs. Finally, she was fully immersed as he continued walking into the pool. Smooth tiles pushed against her back as he pressed her against the side and pushed his cock deeper into her. She kissed him, feeling faint from the intensity of her emotions. She wanted to cry and laugh at the same time. She felt frenzied yet intensely focused. He pulled back and thrust into her. His hot, hard cock stroked inside her.

"Yes." Finally, he was fucking her like she'd wanted, but this time, he'd already taken her close to orgasm several times. It seemed he could do it at will. She didn't have to work at it, or be afraid to lose it.

His long, hard depth thrust into her again. The now familiar waves of pleasure began. He stopped thrusting and lifted her out of the pool, his cock sliding from her body.

She whimpered but trusted he would not leave her wanting. Cool grass caressed her back. He jumped from the pool and carried her to a soft, fluffy blanket lying on a mound of grass. He'd obviously been planning this. He laid her down gently, then prowled over her. As his muscular body covered hers and his cock slid into her, she gasped, knowing that tonight, without doubt, she would experience her first orgasm.

He thrust and she moaned. He spiraled, and intense pleasure swirled through her. She wrapped her legs around him, ready for the pleasure, knowing she would welcome it this time, not run from it.

He thrust faster and faster.

"This is what you want, sweetheart. Fast and hard."

The pleasure rose and the now familiar heat closed around her. She opened to it, welcoming it.

Then he stopped and pulled free.

She stared at him in absolute astonishment, then sat up.

"I . . ." She didn't know what to say. What to ask. But she trusted him to bring her pleasure.

He lay down on the blanket. His cock stood straight up, obviously still wanting her.

He smiled. "Why don't you take control?"

He drew on her elbow and she realized what he was suggesting. She arched her knee over him and lowered her body onto his hot, hard cock. She slid down slowly, loving the feel of it stroking the length of her.

Heat burned through every part of her. She wanted an orgasm. She *needed* an orgasm.

Damn it, she was going to give herself an orgasm.

She lifted her body and dropped down on him again. Pleasure sparked through her. She rocked her pelvis, driving his cock deep inside her.

"Oh, God, you feel good," she murmured.

"So do you."

She rocked back and forth, driving him deeper each time. His lovely cock sent wild, erotic sensations rocketing through her. The heat seared through her, then . . .

Oh God, it was happening!

A feeling like no other blazed through her. She sucked

in a breath, then wailed on a long, quivering eruption of pure bliss.

For the first time she knew—as every nerve ending sizzled in explosive pyrotechnics, and her senses dissolved into a scorching mass of intense physical pleasure.

nine

Hanna stared down at J.M., her eyes wide. He smiled and cupped her cheeks, drawing her to his lips for a gentle kiss.

He slid his hands down her arms to her hips, then over her buttocks, and squeezed. The walls of her vagina compressed around his hard cock, still buried deep inside her, and she gasped as another mind-melting orgasm claimed her.

"Oh, God. Ohhh. . . ." She wailed in complete abandon, riding the wave of bliss.

She sank onto his chest, melting against the muscular planes of his solid body, his hard cock still buried inside her.

"That was so . . . I felt so . . ."

His arms tightened around her in a gentle squeeze as he nuzzled the top of her head.

"That was an orgasm. Just in case you weren't sure."

She laughed, unable to contain the effervescent emotions bubbling within her.

"It was incredible." She realized tears welled in her eyes and she wiped them away. She shifted, aware of his massive erection still inside her. "Now, don't *you* want to . . . ?"

He rolled her over. The blanket, soft and fluffy against her back, contrasted with the solid mass of man on top of her. He pivoted his hips forward, pushing his cock deeper into her, then pivoted back, withdrawing an inch. Then he rocked forward again. She clenched around his marble-hard shaft. Breathing became difficult once again. He swirled his hips and his cock spiraled around, stroking every nerve ending inside her. She gasped, then wailed again as another orgasm flashed through her with blinding intensity.

She lay back, gasping for breath. He kissed one taut nipple, then captured her lips. The pleasant pressure of his mouth released and he smiled at her as he pushed his still hard cock inside, then withdrew it from her spent body.

"But you . . ."

He wrapped his hand around his enormous cock, veins nearly popping across the surface.

"This time was all for you."

He lifted her and carried her into his bedroom and settled her beside him.

This time was all for you.

Hanna woke up with the feel of a hard, warm body

next to hers and the echo of J.M.'s words in her heart. She opened her eyes to see J.M. lying beside her. Her head rested in the crook of his arm and her leg curled over his knees.

She could feel the beat of his heart against her ear. His solid chest rose and fell with his slow and steady breathing.

Sunlight washed across his face. Her gaze danced across his handsome, rugged features, her heart compressing in joy. The world seemed far away as she listened to the beat of his heart, losing herself in the rise and fall of his chest as he drew in slow, even breaths.

A strong, compelling feeling washed over her. Tenderness. Gratitude. Joy. Love.

Love?

Did she love him? The thought startled her. Could it be possible? She had found a new joy in his arms. But that wasn't enough to signify love. Was it?

Barriers had fallen away last night and her heart felt open. Right now, she felt closer to J.M. than she had ever felt to anyone before.

Even Grey.

Ignoring a tiny stab of guilt, she stroked a stray wave of hair from J.M.'s forehead, careful not to wake him. Last night had been incredible. She had never experienced anything so profound.

And he had done it all for her.

She could lie here forever, in the warmth of his arms,

her body pressed against his solid length. Enjoying the rise and fall of his chest against her cheek, the thump of his heart under her ear, the whisper of his pulse through his body.

She loved him. It was as if magic floated around her. Life looked different than it ever had before, filled with possibilities she'd denied herself for too long.

As soon as Hanna opened her door, she knew she was in trouble. The sight of Grey illuminated by her porch light with his knapsack in his hand sent her pulse racing. She'd been struggling all day with how to tell him she was in love with another man.

She also wanted to tell J.M. about Grey, but she hadn't been sure what to say.

My ex-boyfriend is coming to town again and he's spending a couple of nights with me.

She hadn't known how to explain the situation. When she'd discovered Grey was coming to town for the course, it had just seemed reasonable that she let him stay here. She had two bedrooms, all his stuff was here, and this had been his home for the past year.

Oh, yeah, and by the way, he is going to hypnotize me to discover my deepest sexual fantasies.

No, she'd decided she'd just have to explain to Grey how far things had progressed between her and J.M. That she was serious about J.M., and that she couldn't keep seeing Grey. She would let him stay here this time, but he'd have to find somewhere else after this. And as for the hypnosis . . .

As she stared at his handsome, familiar face smiling at her, her heart thumped a little faster.

Good heavens, if she was in love with J.M., why did the sight of Grey send her heartbeat into overdrive?

That was simple. Just because she'd fallen in love with J.M. didn't change the fact that she was still in love with Grey.

But it was time to move on.

He plopped his knapsack and computer bag onto the floor, then drew her into his arms. Thoughts of protest barely reached the surface of her mind before his lips claimed hers and within seconds she was responding to his deep, passionate kiss.

"Grey, I . . . ," she began as he released her.

He grabbed his computer bag and grasped her hand, drawing her along with him to the living room.

"Let's get started," he said. "I've been looking forward to this all week."

He unzipped the bag and tugged out his laptop, then set it on the desk by the window.

"It's been a long day for you," she said, standing beside him, watching him open the device. "With the drive and then your class . . . I thought you'd want to wait until tomorrow."

He pushed the button to start up the computer, then glanced toward her.

"I know it's a little late, but I was really hoping you'd be up to this tonight."

She wrung her hands together.

"Grey, I've been thinking. . . ."

He cupped her shoulders and smiled warmly. His touch threw her off-kilter.

"Honey, I know you must be nervous about this, but don't worry about it. I read this great book about hypnosis, and it looks like it could be a lot of fun. And really helpful."

Before she had a chance to say a thing he continued.

"I found some software that helped me make a recording where I combined music with an underlying pulse of sound to take you into a deep hypnotic state. I talked to the instructor about it—I met with him before class this week—and he thinks it will work quite well. It's almost certain you'll be drawn into a trance right away, rather than having to make several attempts."

He sat down beside her and smiled at her. "You look so worried." He kissed her on the cheek. "Relax. We'll talk about exactly what we're going to do, and I promise I'll stick to what we decide."

She shook her head, feeling like she was being swept away by a raging river current. She had to stick to what she'd decided.

"Grey, I don't want you to hypnotize me." The words came out a little sharp.

His smile faded. She felt compelled to fill the sudden void.

"I know I agreed, but I've changed my mind. Something . . . happened."

Pain washed through his moss green eyes.

"What kind of something?"

But they both knew he knew exactly what had happened.

She sighed. "You know I've been seeing someone else. Well, he and I, when we made love . . ." She almost choked on the words, knowing the painful effect they were having on Grey. "I . . ." She clasped her hands in front of her. "I just realize I have strong feelings for him. I think he—"

"Might be the one?" Grey practically snarled. "I assume you finally had an orgasm. That doesn't mean you're in love with him." His eyes narrowed. "But you don't believe that, do you?"

He grasped her hands in his. "For God's sake, Hanna, give me a chance. I can do the same for you. And even if I can't, I . . ."

His eyes shone with a depth of emotion she'd never seen there before. She could almost swear he'd been about to tell her he loved her.

He kissed her knuckles, his warm lips sending a soft, earnest glow washing through her. "Just think about the year we spent together." He stroked a curl of hair from her cheek, his touch melting her heart. "Isn't that more significant than a mere physical sensation, no matter how exhilarating?"

His words and his touch threatened to overwhelm her. She withdrew her hands from his tender grasp and stood up, shaking her head.

"I can't do this with you. I just can't."

She turned her back on him and started toward the door.

"But, Hanna."

Her hand froze on the doorknob, but she did not turn around.

"I love you," he said.

Tears prickled at her eyes. A part of her wanted to turn around and fling herself into his arms. A saner part insisted she pull open the door and leave. Now.

She turned the knob and exited without looking back. It wasn't until she closed her bedroom door behind her that she sucked in a breath.

Oh, my God, does he really love me?

Hanna spent a restless night tossing and turning, knowing Grey slept only yards away in her guest bedroom, a simple barrier of paint and drywall between them.

Images of Grey's naked, muscular body stretched out in her guest room under the white cotton sheets with tiny

pink rosebuds haunted her. Why was it his intimately familiar, strong hands that she imagined skimming over her
body rather than J.M.'s? Her nipples budded, pushing
against her cotton nightshirt. Why was it Grey's hot, tempting mouth she longed for?

She flung her leg sideways and clung to the pillow by
her side, hugging it like a lover.

Damn it, if she loved J.M. why was she thinking
about Grey?

Idiot. She knew what the problem was.

First, she knew she couldn't be in love with J.M. Not
yet, anyway. And her intellect told her that having an orgasm with a man didn't have anything to do with loving
him. But her heart told her anyone who was in synch
with her enough to be able to take her to her bliss—to
help her past whatever blocks had been stopping her—had
to be someone very special to her.

J.M. had an insight into the inner workings of her
psyche that had allowed her to achieve an awesome break-
through. She knew her inability to achieve orgasm was
far more than a matter of physical pleasure. On some
level, she never allowed herself to have what she really
wanted. She always took a safe course, settling for what
she knew she could achieve. Like her coffee shop. She
could manage a business. She was good at it and made a
fine profit. But it wasn't a challenge.

The only thing she had continued to strive for that

she didn't know for sure she could achieve—because on some level she had lost hope long ago—was that all-elusive orgasm. Now that J.M. had shown her the way, she wanted to keep on going. Embracing the ecstasy.

But what if she could only do it with J.M.?

If she was in love with J.M., and if he loved her in return—and that was a big "if"—then everything was great, but . . . the voice of intellect reminded her that love and great sex didn't always go hand in hand.

Fear careened through her at the thought that she might only be able to achieve ecstasy in J.M.'s arms. Maybe only he could understand what she needed, with that in-tuitive ability of his.

She heard a door open and footsteps in the hall.

Grey.

He walked toward her room and her breath caught. Was he going to come into her room? Seduce her with gentle words of love?

She heard the light switch click in the bathroom next to her room, then the water run. A moment later, his foot-steps sounded back down the hall, then his door closed.

He'd probably been filling the water glass he always kept by the bed when he slept. Had he put on his robe before he'd left his room or had he walked her hall naked? If she'd gotten up and peeked outside, would she have seen his broad, naked chest, sprinkled with dark hair ta-pering down his tightly ridged stomach? Would she have seen his immense cock swinging from side to side, bouncing on the heavy sacs behind?

She sucked in a breath, feeling the moisture ooze between her legs. She closed her eyes, trying to calm her thunderous heartbeat, knowing if she stood up and walked into his room, then slipped into his bed, he would welcome her. His cock would harden at the feel of her in his arms. She could imagine his long cock, hard as steel, sliding into her. Her finger slid down to her moist opening and she stroked the slick flesh. He would drive into her, hard. Her thunderous heartbeat pounded in her ears as she breathed rapidly, her finger stroking over her clit, sending sparks of pleasure through her.

She would roll him over and slam down on him, then ride him . . . up and down . . . his sweet cock gliding into her over and over again . . . until she screeched in orgasm. Her clit, hard and swollen beneath her fingers, sent wild tendrils of intense sensation coiling through her body. She pushed two fingers inside. Waves of heat pulsed toward her. She stroked harder on her clit, vibrating her finger back and forth, and thrust her fingers inside. The waves swelled . . . then receded. She stroked and thrust, her thighs tightening, her heart thudding, but nothing she did brought it closer.

She imagined Grey pounding into her. Imagined him bringing her to orgasm. But the dream didn't turn into reality.

Finally, she flopped back on the bed in failure, gasping for breath, her hand aching.

Oh, God, what if she couldn't achieve an orgasm again?

Hanna awoke the next morning with the sheets coiled around her legs like a rope. She was needy and frustrated. She heard water running and realized Grey was taking a shower.

Thoughts of him soaping his tall, well-sculpted body, his hands running over the masculine planes, ignited the heat within her again. She leaped from her bed and pranced into her en suite bathroom, where she quickly showered and pulled on her work clothes.

When she entered the kitchen, Grey was making a pot of coffee.

"Hi there. Would you like one of my famous ham and cheese omelets?"

He looked so attractive standing there all freshly washed and shaved, the tangy smell of his familiar aftershave tantalizing. The sunlight from the window glinted off his sandy brown hair as it curled around his ears in waves. He held her yellow plastic mixing bowl in one hand and a package of eggs in the other.

She had always loved his omelets, especially with his signature dash of spices.

"No, thanks."

"But you don't have to be at the shop until nine thirty."

"I need to be in early today," she lied. "Are you leaving this afternoon?"

He had been going to stay until tomorrow, but under the circumstances . . .

"I was going to stick around until after dinner, if that's okay with you."

Not really. She intended to avoid him as much as possible, not wanting to give him—or her—any chance of falling into the other's arms.

"Do you want me to drive you?"

"No, thanks. It's a beautiful day. I'll walk."

He knew she always walked, so they both knew he'd only asked her so he could spend more time with her. She felt callous turning him down, but she had to get away. His presence was throwing her way off balance.

She strode out the door. As soon as she got around the corner from her house, she flicked open her cell phone and dialed J.M.'s number.

ten

The doorbell rang. J.M. knew that would be Hanna. He set the last roll in the basket, then headed for the door.

The anticipation of seeing his lovely Hanna made him smile, despite the concern that had been simmering through him since her early-morning call. She had been anxious to see him today, so he'd invited her over for lunch, sensing she would prefer privacy rather than a public restaurant. Luckily, since Grey Bennet had asked to reschedule their 11:00 A.M. meeting, J.M. had had time to drive home and prepare lunch ahead of time.

Grey had called him on Monday to move their appointment up a day—to yesterday before the course. He'd wanted to do the hypnosis Tuesday night after the course and he wanted to go over some questions with J.M. beforehand.

J.M. liked the man. He sensed the depth of Grey's

love for his woman and admired what Grey had. J.M. hoped the hypnosis had worked out well for them both.

As J.M. crossed the living room, he saw Hanna's shadow in the frosted glass sidelight. Right after his second class, he'd headed home and pulled together a simple lunch of cheese, bread, and cold sliced meat. He didn't know how hungry Hanna would be, especially since she was clearly unnerved about something.

Since his Wednesday schedule was light—only two morning meetings and the one-hour office time for student appointments—he usually spent the afternoon writing. Today, however, if Hanna needed to talk, he would dedicate the time to her.

"Hi, sweetheart. Come in."

She stepped inside and followed him to the living room, where he'd set out plates, the food, and a big pitcher of water.

"I thought we'd be more comfortable in here." He gestured toward the couch. He retrieved the basket of rolls from the kitchen, then sat in the chair across from her. He felt she might need some distance.

They'd only talked briefly since their incredible love-making last Friday. Afterward, he'd sensed her confusion and the tumultuous emotions whirling through her. He'd dropped into the coffee shop the next day and she'd joined him for tea and one of her delicious banana nut muffins, but she still seemed tense. Achieving a sexual climax after not being able to do so for such a long time meant she'd breached some huge emotional block. It might take her a while to adapt.

Now, however, her energy seemed way off balance. She seemed to be struggling with some issue, and he could tell she had something to tell him.

"Lunch looks great," she said.

He watched her nibble at the food, not consuming very much. She sipped her glass of water, then sat with her hands clasped in her lap.

"Hanna, what's wrong?"

"I, uh . . ." She smiled at him. "Well, I want to thank you again for the other night. It was . . ." She shrugged. ". . . incredible."

He smiled, remembering her naked body shifting on his, then her long wail as she reached the pinnacle.

"My pleasure."

She picked up a celery stick and nibbled the end absently.

"Hanna, are you afraid you can only orgasm with me?"

She stared at him, her wide eyes showing that his intuition had given him the right answer—and unnerved her a little.

"I . . ." She nodded and stared at her hands, folded in her lap. "I am worried about that." She gazed at him again. "It was so great with you. And you put *me* in control—that was such a great thing—but it was still you who . . . you know . . . brought it all together."

"That doesn't mean you can't have an orgasm anytime you want."

"I tried last night . . . I mean, on my own . . . but I . . . couldn't."

He took her hand.

"That's all right. We'll work on that. And the more we make love and you find that place, the more confident you'll be, and the easier it will become."

Her gaze ricocheted to his. "But what if . . . ?" She paused.

"What if what?"

"Well, you and I are involved now, but . . . how do I know . . . ?"

"That you can't with someone else?" He smiled. "Do you have someone else in mind?"

He was joking, but the strained look in her eyes gave him his answer. Jealousy, an alien emotion to him, knocked him a hearty blow in the chest.

"Hanna, *is* there someone else?"

"No." She pinched her fingers together. "I mean there was, before I met you. I told you about him. We broke up two months ago."

"He's the one you met with the other day." He placed his hand on his knee. "Is he trying to get back together with you?"

"He hasn't come out and asked, but I'm almost certain he wants to."

"Tell me, why did you two break up?" he asked.

"We weren't in love."

That wasn't true, but he sensed she didn't think she was lying. As he read her face and her energy, he realized she had believed it when she'd broken up with the man, but right now she had doubts.

J.M.'s gut clenched. Was she here to end it with him?

"The thing is," she continued, "he's in town and he needed a place to stay."

"He's staying with you." It wasn't a question. He knew.

She nodded. "But he's just sleeping there." She sucked in a breath. "Not with me. I mean, he's in the guest room. It's like this. He went to New York on a six-month contract right after we broke up, so I let him leave his stuff at my place. Now he needs to come back for two days a week. I said he could stay this week, but now that you and I are involved, it's not really appropriate. I'm going to tell him that he'll have to find somewhere else. For the other days."

"Why are you telling me this?"

"I just wanted you to know that he's at my house. Last night and today. And that this is the only time, now that I'm involved with you."

J.M. sat back and watched her. She'd gone out with this guy for a long time. She had believed they were in love—and a part of her wondered about it now. And now that she'd experienced an orgasm with J.M. . . .

"You want to know if you can experience an orgasm with him."

Her face flushed red. She stared at him, wide-eyed, but she did not deny it.

She was only holding off because she was involved with J.M. now, but it would be good for her to know. It would alleviate her doubts. Give her more confidence. If she stayed with him and never found out the truth, he knew she'd always wonder.

It wasn't right to hold her back.

"You should do it."

Hanna couldn't go back to work. She hurt too much inside. She couldn't believe that J.M. could so casually suggest she sleep with another man, *especially* one with whom she had such history.

She called Jessica, whom she knew had only morning classes on Monday and Wednesday, to take the rest of her shift, then headed home.

Would Grey still be there? Good heavens, what would she say to him?

After he had proclaimed his love for her last night. After J.M. had declared that she should sleep with Grey.

Oh, God, she was so confused.

As she walked past her neighbor's house with the tall cedar hedge, she noticed that Grey's silver Corvette was not in her driveway. She should be relieved, but she wasn't. After last night, and the way she'd made it clear she'd moved on, he was probably gone forever.

Her heart ached at the thought of never seeing Grey again, and another pang of guilt stabbed through her.

She unlocked the front door and stepped from the warmth of the afternoon into her cool foyer. Sunlight streamed across the living room carpet. She slumped into the easy chair, then flopped her feet on the ottoman and sat staring straight ahead.

When had life gotten so complicated?

She pulled the folded cotton-knit blanket from the couch and tugged it over her shoulders. Tears welled in her eyes.

J.M. had said it was so she could grow, but no guy told a woman to go sleep with her ex-boyfriend if he really cared about her.

Correction. She didn't doubt J.M. cared about her, but if he really *loved* her he wouldn't tell her to go have sex with another man.

Last night she'd been worried about loving two men, and today she didn't have a single one to love her back.

Grey was everything she wanted in a man, except that he had never said he loved her. But now he had said it.

And now, despite J.M.'s patience and intuition, it seemed she had the same problem with him. In other circumstances, she might assume she was just expecting too much too soon, but the fact that he was pushing her at another man sent a pretty clear message.

And now she'd hurt Grey and he'd left.

Tears spilled freely now and she grabbed a box of tissues and blew her nose.

Grey pulled into the driveway at Hanna's wondering if she was home yet. He'd almost decided to head straight back to New York after his meeting with his boss at the local office, but he didn't want to leave it this way with Hanna.

It wasn't fair. Now that this new guy had taken her to orgasm—the guy must be a genius in the ways of women and sex—it would be practically impossible to convince her that she and Grey were meant for each other. He loved her, and he knew she loved him—she just wouldn't admit it.

He could wait for the relationship to fizzle out—maybe that's what he'd have to do—but he didn't want to wait, and he didn't want Hanna to get hurt. And she would be hurt, because he knew she'd totally convince herself she was in love with this new guy and be devastated when it turned out otherwise.

Grey wanted to avoid that. He couldn't bear to see her hurt.

He unlocked the front door and stepped inside. In the dim light of the living room, he saw a hazy shape, then realized the shape was a blanket-clad Hanna, slumped in

the chair, fast asleep, her legs stretched out on the ottoman.

As his eyes adapted to the low light, he realized there
were little white balls crumpled around her. At the sight
of the box of tissues by her hand, he realized she'd been
crying.

What the hell?

Had the bastard she'd started dating dumped her already?

He knelt beside the chair and stroked her arm. Her
eyes opened.

"Oh, Grey." She threw her arms around his neck and
he held her close. "I thought you'd gone."

"It's okay, sweetheart. I'm here."

She stroked his cheek, her soft hand running across
his unshaven skin sending gentle pulses of need through
him.

"Are you okay?"

She nodded.

"What about the other guy?" he asked.

Her face crumpled and tears sprang from her eyes.
That's all he needed to know. It was over between them.
The joy that blossomed in his chest converged with the
compassion he felt for her pain.

He wanted to gather her into his arms and make it all
better. He wanted to show her how much he loved her so
she had no doubt in her mind.

He wrapped his arms around her and pulled her close.

The feel of her soft, warm body against his made his heart thrum.

He stroked her silky hair and held her snugly against him. After a few moments, her sobs softened and she clung to him. He kissed her temple. She gazed up at him with shining eyes, and he captured her lips.

"I love you so much, Hanna." He'd never said it before last night, but now he wanted to say it all the time.

He felt a little guilty, because he couldn't bring himself to tell her about his issue yet—the time just wasn't right—but he couldn't stop himself from telling her how he felt about her.

He kissed her forehead, then her cheek, then took her lips again. "I love you."

Hanna's heart ached at his words.

"Grey, I think . . ."

He stared at her, his moss green eyes intense.

"Maybe you just think you love me because you're afraid of losing me," she continued.

He looked a little startled.

"And why would I be afraid of losing you if I didn't love you?"

She hesitated.

"Because you know me," she said. "You're comfortable with me. Because I'm convenient."

The grin turning up his lips surprised her.

He nudged his forehead against hers, his grin broadening.

"Hanna, you are many things to me, but convenient is certainly not one of them."

"But—"

"Don't get me wrong. I love studying ancient sexual rituals, making love to you long into the night, and trying different sexual techniques, all in hopes of helping bring you pleasure, but I definitely wouldn't define that as convenient."

A tear swelled from her eye and streamed down her face.

"Oh, God, I'm a pain in the ass."

He kissed the tears away.

"No, you're the woman I love. Hanna, believe me. I'm not just saying it to win you back. I'm saying it because it's true. I love you."

Her heart swelled. He really did. She could see it shining in his eyes.

"Grey, I love you, too." She felt so close to him now, and she wanted to be closer. She drew his hand to her breast, pressing it against her soft flesh. "Make love to me."

He drew her into a tight embrace and kissed her passionately, then drew away.

"Hanna, there is nothing I would rather do than make love to you right now . . . to show you how much I love you . . . but . . ." He stroked her cheek with a tenderness that melted her heart. "The next time I make love to you, I want to make you come."

Her stomach tightened. What if she didn't come with

Grey? Especially now that he'd told her he loved her. It would devastate him.

"What about the hypnosis? Why don't we try that?"

Grey sat back in the chair and tried to relax, even though the thought of what they were about to do had his heart palpitating with excitement. He mentally went through the preparations he'd made for the session they had planned for yesterday.

"I'm going to play some music which will take you into a deep hypnotic state."

Grey was glad he'd found the software to make the tape. It made use of soft music with underlying pulses designed to take the brain into a receptive state. It also made use of a set induction script done in a canned voice. Jeremy had offered to make a tape to take Hanna through the induction, but for some reason, Grey wasn't comfortable with the thought of the other man's voice being part of their session.

"After a while, I'll start to talk. You will be very receptive to any suggestions I make. Nothing I say will make you do something you don't really want to do. The intent of today is to relax you and lower your subconscious barriers so you can express your fantasies. We'll go after one fantasy you'd like to experience. Then I'll bring you out of the trance and we'll talk about it."

"Okay, why don't we do it now?"

His heart rate leaped. He'd been longing to take her through some wild sexual fantasy, anticipating it with great relish. Hell, he'd used it as *his* sexual fantasy ever since he'd started reading the hypnosis book.

Could he do it now? He'd been planning on finding out her fantasy, then preparing a script, like the examples in the book.

At the thought of Hanna lying naked on the couch, squirming under the effect of his words, aroused beyond reason, because he'd talked her through her deepest sexual fantasy, his cock pushed against the confines of his jeans.

"So you want me to ask you about your fantasy, then take you through it?" He wanted to make sure they understood each other completely.

She smiled.

"That's right."

Adrenaline pulsed through him. This would involve some quick thinking on his part, but he would definitely figure it out.

He pulled out his laptop to start the background music with the appropriate underlying pulses to quickly take her into a hypnotic state.

"Okay, close your eyes and relax," he said.

She shifted on the couch, tucking a pillow behind her back and stretching her legs out along the couch. She tucked another pillow behind her head.

He watched her, stretched out on the couch, her eyes closed. He wanted to take her in his arms and kiss her . . .

to carry her to the bed, strip off her clothes, and ravage her . . . but he resisted. The promise of the fascinating possibilities to come kept him planted in the chair. He wondered what her fantasy would be. More, he longed to see her writhe in orgasm, her body quivering in blissful release.

He let the music and the canned voice from his software program talk her through the induction. Her breathing deepened and her body seemed limp and relaxed. Could she really be in a deep hypnotic state?

The canned voice stopped, but the soft music continued, and would continue indefinitely. It was time for him to begin. He cleared his throat and referred to the notes he'd prepared from the various scripts in the hypnosis book.

"Hanna, I am going to ask you what kind of sexual fantasy you would like to experience. I want you to put aside any inhibitions that are stopping you from expressing your deepest, wildest fantasy. Something that you've longed to experience, even if you haven't consciously realized it. Allow it to bubble up from your subconscious. Accept it, no matter how surprising it is to you, then tell me what it is. You will find it easy to talk to me about your private thoughts and fantasies. Any fear or awkwardness will fade away and it will become easy to tell me what you want. Remember, you are safe and loved. I will not judge. I will find your fantasy just as exciting and arousing as you do."

He wondered what fantasy lurked in her highly imaginative but controlled mind. Whatever it was, he couldn't wait to find out.

"I'm going to touch you on the shoulder in a moment. When I do, lift your head, open your eyes, and tell me in a clear, loud voice what your sexual fantasy is."

He knew from the books he'd read that she would probably provide a minimal answer using few words.

"If I ask you questions, answer them clearly."

He leaned forward and touched her on the shoulder. Excitement zoomed through him as she lifted her head and opened her eyes, then stared straight ahead with a vacant expression.

"Bikers."

eleven

Grey stared at Hanna, sitting on the couch, her eyes gazing straight ahead. He waited for more, but that's all she said.

"You want to be a biker chick?"

"No."

He raised his eyebrows.

"You want to make love to a biker?"

"No."

"What do you want to have happen with a biker?"

"I want to be ravaged."

"Oh. . . ."

He shook his head. His demure little Hanna wanted to be grabbed by some hulky biker in black leather and chains and be fucked silly?

In the safeness of her own fantasies, of course.

He smiled. *Well, why the hell not?*

Hanna drew in a deep breath. As soon as Grey's words told her to allow her deepest fantasies to bubble up from her subconscious, she'd felt something secret and forbidden creep through her. Awareness of a hidden fantasy pulsed through her—one that would sear the edges of her consciousness. He had released the hidden genie, so to speak, and it filled her with overwhelming desire.

Half of her wanted to tell him what she wanted, in vivid detail, but the other half was content to just relax and wait for him to ask. . . .

Grey rubbed his hand over his chin.

The hypnosis book had suggested that the partner being hypnotized get undressed before a session where there would be a sexual fantasy, but he and Hanna hadn't planned this ahead of time. He wanted her to be comfortable and able to do what she needed to do.

She had told him to go ahead with whatever would make the session better, but he wanted to be sure.

"Hanna, in a moment I'm going to start the fantasy, but first I'm going to ask you to remove your clothes. Are you comfortable with doing that?"

"Yes."

Excitement swirled inside him. He sucked in a deep breath, longing to see her lovely naked body once again.

"Stand up, take off your clothes, then lay them on the chair. After that, lie down on the couch, close your eyes, and relax again."

She stood up and pulled her T-shirt over her head, revealing her lovely breasts encased in a turquoise satin and lace bra. She folded her T-shirt neatly and laid it on the armchair beside the couch. She unfastened her bra and slid it off. Her round, firm breasts bounced slightly as she folded her bra, then set it on top of her shirt. His gaze remained on her dusky, delightful nipples as she released the button on her jeans, drew down the zipper, then dropped them to the floor. She stepped out of them, then leaned over to pick them up, allowing him a lovely view of her round, firm derriere, naked except for a small triangle of turquoise lace at the waist strap of her thong. Next, she shimmied out of her thong. She folded the jeans and placed them and her thong on the chair.

She lay down on the couch again and linked her hands as she rested them on her stomach. His gaze shifted from her perky nipples to her delicious naked pussy. He longed to lean toward her and pet the lovely, silken curls, or to tweak her tight nipples between his fingertips. But he leaned back, drawing in a lungful of air, calming his intense cravings.

"Okay, now I'd like you to imagine you're standing at the side of a long, lonely stretch of highway, beside your car. It's broken down and you're not sure what to do. You tried calling for help on your cell phone, but there is no signal. The sun is going to set soon, and you're getting a little nervous. You've been stranded for about an hour and you really want someone to drive by and help you. Listen to the sounds around you. There are the sounds of birds in the trees and crickets in the grass."

He paused, giving her time to build a mental image.

"As you listen carefully, you hear a sound in the distance. An engine, but not a car or truck. You think it might be a motorcycle. You stare down the long, straight road and in the distance you see it. A motorcycle heading in your direction. Excitement curls through you, and a little fear, knowing a biker might be dangerous, but deep inside you know you are safe."

He smiled as he noticed her nipples hardening into tight buds.

Hanna's whole body tingled with excitement. She could see the big black chrome-encrusted motorcycle heading her way. A man, dressed in black leather and wearing a black helmet, rode the beast. Closer and closer he came. The engine roared in her ears. She knew she should hide from this dangerous man, but her legs wouldn't move. She stared in fascination as he loomed closer.

There was always the chance he would drive right by.

"The biker sees you and pulls over, then pulls off his helmet and goggles."

The man pulled off the road in a swirl of dust and pulled up beside her car. He tossed his goggles aside and tugged off his helmet, revealing dark, wavy hair, tied back in a ponytail. Several strands curled over his shoulder, reaching almost to his waist. Her fingers itched to tug off the leather strap binding it and run through the long, lustrous waves.

"He is tall and extremely handsome. He says it's dangerous for a beautiful woman to be all alone on such a lonely stretch of road."

His dark eyes pierced hers as he said it, assessing her. She stood frozen, unsure what to do. What to say.

He looked so much like Grey. Just as sexy and alluring. Although she felt fear, she also felt safe, knowing he wouldn't hurt her. Yet that strange sense of danger heightened her excitement.

"His gaze rakes up and down your body and you find it strangely exciting."

Her body tingled as his gaze raked down her chest, resting on her breasts, watching the nipples rise through her white cotton camisole. Why had she worn such a skimpy top? She never wore things like this. Especially without a bra. And the fabric was so thin. The outlines of her nipples showed clearly through the fabric and she was sure he could see the darker color of her tight aureoles right through it.

His gaze continued downward, caressing her legs, most of which were visible with the extremely short skirt she wore.

"He climbs off his bike and approaches you. You are frozen to the spot, wanting to back away but unable to move your legs."

As he approached, Hanna's excitement grew. With his sculpted facial features, his strong, broad shoulders, his masculine presence . . . she wanted him to grab her and . . .

"He grasps your shoulders and pulls you against him, then kisses you. His tongue invades your mouth, stroking and pulsing against yours. To your own shock, you respond, pushing your tongue into his mouth."

The feel of her body pressed tight against his, of his tongue pushing into her mouth in an almost violent invasion, sent her pulse skyrocketing. She pushed her tongue into his mouth, overwhelmed by the shocking need to taste him, to possess him. This man was a total stranger. Dangerous . . . Frightening . . . Yet an irresistible urge to be possessed by him pulsed through her.

His arms tightened around her, crushing her against his broad, muscular chest. She could feel his cock bulging through his leather pants, pushing against her stomach.

Oh, God, she wanted to drop to her knees and release his zipper, then reach in for the prize.

"He lifts you up and places you on his bike, in front of him."

She felt the leather seat slide along her thighs as he eased her onto his bike. The curved seat settled between her legs, only the thin white cotton of her panties separating her moist flesh from the hot leather. Hot from his body, which was pressed against her. Heat swarmed her senses, washing over her.

"Don't worry about having no helmet or the fact you're in front of him. In this fantasy, it works and you're perfectly safe."

She didn't need a helmet. Driving on this high-powered

machine was perfectly safe. It was the man who caused her concern . . . and excitement.

"He positions your hands on his legs and you hang on as he starts up the motorcycle and pulls onto the road."

She had to stop herself from stroking his solid, muscular legs through the supple leather. Her fingers wrapped around his thighs as the machine roared to life and thrust forward.

"You are thrilled by the feel of the wind in your hair, and the handsome biker behind you."

One of his hands draped casually around her waist, holding her close to his broad chest. Where was he taking her?

"You feel his hand stroke over your stomach as he lifts your shirt and draws it over your head. You didn't wear a bra today."

She felt his big fingers slide over her rib cage.

With the fabric gone, she felt the wind against her naked breasts. It was more gentle than she would have thought, caressing rather than whipping against her, even though they moved at a tremendous speed.

"His hand strokes over your right breast, then your left. Your nipples tighten."

As Grey watched, her nipples did tighten. He licked his lips as he watched them, along with the goose bumps quivering along her breasts.

She was so clearly turned on. He desperately wanted to touch her. Or watch her touch herself. He realized he hadn't given her instructions to allow her to touch herself and, in the trance, she wouldn't. Her limbs would lie limp beside her unless he instructed otherwise.

"Hanna, you can move your body or limbs however you want to enhance this experience. If you want to touch yourself, you can."

Her hands moved to her breasts and she stroked them, then cupped them in her hands.

"With his free hand, he touches your nipples, pinching them between his fingers."

Her fingers dabbed at her nipples, then she squeezed them between her fingertips. His cock swelled at the sight.

"His hand slips down your stomach and moves over your skirt."

Her hand slid down over her belly and over her naked thighs.

"It's very short. He pulls it up and his hand dips into your panties."

Her hand slid over her mound.

"You cling to his legs, unwilling to let go to stop his caresses. Realizing you don't want to. His finger strokes over your pussy and dips inside. You are very wet."

Her finger stroked her slit, then dipped inside. She moaned softly. His gaze remained locked on her hand.

"He strokes inside your pussy, sending delightful waves of pleasure through you."

Oh, God, she could feel his hand on her hot, dripping pussy. His fingers stroking inside her.

She should stop this. Struggle against him. But she couldn't.

She didn't want to.

"Now he moves his finger to your clitoris. As he strokes it, you find you're breathing heavily, wanting him to do more."

She leaned against him, her head falling back on his shoulder, his cheek pressed against hers as his finger stroked over her clit. Glorious sensations spiraled through her.

"You can feel his erection pushing at your back. You push back against it. His hand moves away and you know he's unfastening his leather pants."

She could feel his fingers working at his pants. In a moment, his big, hard cock would be free. Would he take her right here on the bike as they sped along the highway?

Oh, God, I hope so.

"His hand returns to your panties and he rips them away, tossing them to the wind. Now your pussy is fully exposed."

She gasped. The cool breeze rushed across her . . . pussy. She squeezed her legs, pressing her naked pussy tight against the leather seat, the ridges pressing into her, stimulating her with the vibration of the machine.

Her breathing increased.

"He lifts you up a little and you feel his cock slide under you, between the leather seat and your pussy."

The long, hard rod slid under her, stroking along her wet slit.

"You squirm on it, feeling how hard it is. How long it is. You know he's going to push it inside you. You know he's going to fuck you. You feel a little fearful at the dangerous situation, but you are so excited . . . and deep down, you know you are safe."

A quiver of fear danced along her spine, but she ignored it, knowing he wouldn't hurt her. Knowing she could enjoy this.

She tilted her pelvis forward and back, stroking his rock-hard cock with her wet pussy.

"He strokes your breasts again, then flicks your clit as he pushes his cock forward and backward."

As he stroked her slit with his rock-hard cock, she moaned.

"He angles you forward and you know what he's going to do next."

His hand pressed her bottom forward until she leaned over the handlebars, breasts swaying in the breeze.

"His cock slides inside you. It feels *so* good."

She felt his cock nudge her opening, then slide inside. She gasped at the intense pleasure.

"You love the feel of that rock-hard cock inside you."

Oh, God, the feel of that long, hard cock sliding inside her was incredible.

At Hanna's gasp, a painful jolt of need spiked through Grey. He watched as her fingers stroked her pussy, her legs lying wide apart. She moaned a little and his cock pulsed with need. He had to stop himself from ripping off his clothes and climbing on top of her.

This whole situation was intensely exciting.

"He starts thrusting inside you and an exhilarating tension builds within you. The pleasure is undeniable and potent. And very illicit, making it all the more exciting. He thrusts and you moan."

A low, audible moan escaped her lips. He ran his hand over his bulge, wishing he could find relief yet wanting this to go on and on. To bring Hanna to orgasm.

"The pleasure builds as he thrusts into you. You know you can come anytime you want, but you decide not to just yet."

He didn't want to make her think she couldn't climax, but he wanted to build the heat. To make it better for her.

Hanna felt pressure build inside her. Pleasure washed through every part of her. She knew she could ride the waves to orgasm as the sexy biker thrust into her again and again, but she decided to wait. To let it build.

"He thrusts . . . harder and faster."

His big cock pounded into her, gliding in and out of her slick vagina, setting off fiery explosions along her nerve endings.

"You can feel him tense; then he comes inside you . . ."

Oh, God, he was coming.

"... grunting and spurting hot liquid into your wet pussy...."

She could feel it. A hot fountain spewing inside her.

"... You can't hold back any longer. The orgasm washes over you."

Pleasure catapulted through her, driving her over the edge to that delightful abyss.

"Oh, God, yes," she wailed. "I'm ... I'm coming."

Grey nearly exploded at the sound of her orgasmic release.

She'd come right on cue. He felt powerful and immensely satisfied knowing he'd been able to bring her to orgasm—and just with words.

Hanna tied her robe tightly around her waist as she hurried to the door. She pulled it open to see Grace smiling at her.

"Good morning, sleepyhead. Aren't you ready yet?"

"Ready?" Hanna stared at her blankly, then her hand flew to her mouth as she remembered today was their day to run. She'd asked Grace if they could postpone to Thursday when she'd first agreed to do the hypnosis with Grey, so she could sleep in on Wednesday.

"You forgot again, didn't you?" Grace accused as she stepped past Hanna and dropped her bag and running shoes on the floor, then kicked off her sandals. "Is there coffee?"

"Not yet." Grey's voice sounded behind Hanna. His

hands came to rest on her shoulders and he kissed her cheek. "Good morning, sweetheart."

She could feel the heat of his body so close behind her. Grace's eyebrows raised slightly.

"Grey. Nice to see you again."

"You, too, Grace." He stroked Hanna's cheek. "Should I go make some coffee?"

"Would you?" Grace smiled.

Once the kitchen door closed behind him, Grace grabbed Hanna's arm and led her to the couch, dragging her to a sitting position beside her.

"So, are you and Grey back together again? I thought things were going so well between you and the new guy. What happened?"

"I told him that Grey was staying here and . . . he said he knew I was worried about whether I could . . . you know, have an orgasm . . . with Grey. . . ."

Grace's eyes narrowed. "Why would he think you were worried about that?"

"Well, he and I . . . *did* . . . so—"

"'Did' as in you had an orgasm with the new guy?"

Hanna nodded. Grace's face broke into a big smile and she threw her arms around Hanna.

"Honey, that's great."

"What's great?" Grey asked as he brought a tray of cups filled with steaming coffee, plus a pitcher of cream and a sugar bowl. He set the tray on the table.

"Just sister talk," Grace said. She added sugar and

cream to her coffee, then took a sip. "So, Sis . . ." She glanced at her watch. "You better get a move on if we're going to do that run today."

Hanna took a sip of her black coffee, then nodded her head. She couldn't ditch Grace again.

Ten minutes later, they were running through the park, along the paved path by the river. Sunlight glittered on the water. The birds twittered in the tall trees shading their path, and the bright yellow daylilies swayed in the breeze.

"To recap," Grace said, "you had an orgasm with this new guy and now you've ditched him for Grey?"

"That's not it at all," Hanna defended. "As I told you, when I mentioned that Grey was staying with me, he figured I was concerned that—"

"I know. You couldn't O with Grey. That seems like an odd thing to come up in the conversation."

"Well, J.M. is different. He's very in tune with people. It's like he can read minds or something. The next thing I knew, he was telling me that I should go give it a try with Grey. To find out."

Grace grunted. "It sounds like this guy has issues of his own. So you ditched the guy and went back to Grey?"

"I haven't broken up with J.M."

"But you slept with Grey."

"Yes, but I didn't *sleep* with Grey."

"Huh?"

Hanna sighed.

"Grey really wanted to help me . . . you know . . . climax. He's been talking to the instructor of that course you told me about—Grey's taking the course—and he wanted to try this thing on me."

"What kind of *thing*?"

"Nothing weird, exactly. He wanted to hypnotize me . . . to find out what sexual fantasies I have."

"And?"

"Uh . . . well, we found out, then he . . . uh . . . led me through it."

"Led you through it? Oh, I like that. So he brought it to life while you were in a trance. I would *love* to try that." She grinned widely. "So what was your fantasy?"

Hanna felt the heat of a blush color her cheeks at the memory of the wild biker fantasy her mind had conjured up—a fantasy she hadn't even known about until last night's session. The thought that Grey knew about it, too, made her cheeks burn hotter.

Hanna pursed her lips. She was absolutely *not* ready to share that fantasy with her sister.

"That's not important. What is important is that . . ." Hanna gazed at her sister, a silly grin claiming her lips.

"Oh, my God. It worked, didn't it?"

"Spectacularly."

Grace nodded like a little bobble-head doll. "Okay. So where does that leave us? Do you still love Grey?"

Hanna's heart swelled at the way he'd made her feel cherished and totally loved last night. He'd murmured sweet words of love in her ear and held her all night long.

"Yes. And he told me he loves me, too."

Grace's eyebrows arched upward. "Really? That man must have gotten past some huge issues. That's great." She rested her hand on Hanna's. "Well, there's no problem too big if you're in love."

Hanna bit her lower lip. It should be that simple, but when she thought about accepting Grey back into her life . . . being a couple again . . . her thoughts turned to J.M. He'd upset her yesterday, but she couldn't forget how his patient, loving way had helped her achieve her first orgasm. Ever. He understood what a woman wanted and needed. But more, he seemed to see into her soul.

Her chest tightened at the thought of losing him.

"Except that . . ." She stared at Grace with wide eyes. "I think I'm in love with J.M., too."

twelve

Hanna knocked on J.M.'s door, her heart thumping in her chest.

The late-afternoon sun cast long shadows across the ground as a bird hopped along the lawn with a berry gripped tightly in its beak.

She had left work as soon as the afternoon rush died down. The thirty-minute walk to J.M.'s had seemed like an eternity.

Her hands clenched at her sides.

What would she say to him? How could she tell him she was still in love with Grey? Should she tell J.M. she loved him, too? In fact, she wasn't even sure if she did love J.M. Maybe her feelings for him were just infatuation, or intense feelings of gratitude.

The door opened and J.M. stood there, devastatingly handsome in his faded denim jeans riding low on his hips, his shirt hanging open. Her fingers longed to reach out and stroke his ridged, well-defined abs. She could imagine stroking his firm, masculine flesh, her fingertips gliding over his rock-hard muscles, traveling down to the sprinkling of hair below his navel that arrowed downward and disappeared beneath the denim.

She licked her lips.

"Hanna. I'm glad you're here." He pulled the door open and she stepped inside. The door clicked closed behind her.

"J.M., we need to talk. I—"

Before she could finish the sentence, she felt herself pulled against J.M.'s broad, hard chest as his lips captured hers.

His fingers stroked through her hair, his other hand pressed firmly against her back, holding her close. Her breasts blossomed with heat at the contact of his masculine body pressed tightly against hers.

The afternoon sunlight danced across his face, and her heart filled with an overwhelming sense of longing. The world, and all the hard questions that so desperately needed answers just a moment ago, faded away. Her heart swelled with . . . it felt like love.

But how could she love two men?

As his hungry mouth devoured hers, all her thoughts settled on this one man wrapped around her. His chest rose and fell against hers as he breathed. The hair on her arms prickled to attention, sending shivers along her skin.

His warm, strong hands cupped her cheeks and his

kisses turned more potent, sending need thrumming through her. Her breasts swelled and her insides tightened.

The hypnosis last night had shocked her. Not what she'd fantasized about—though that had been surprising and outrageously sexy—but the yearning she had uncovered deep inside. To be wild. Free. Uninhibited.

To unleash her inner vixen.

She took his hand and drew it to her breast. He cupped it, his fingers curling around her and squeezing gently.

Her nipples puckered and she backed up until the solid oak door pressed against her back, her inhibitions washed away by the startling need flooding through her body.

Her hand fumbled between them and she tugged her denim skirt upward. She grasped his hand and drew it downward. At the brush of his fingers against her sensitive inner thighs, right below her panties, she sucked in a breath.

"God, you're sexy," he said in a ragged voice.

His fingers slid upward, then stroked along her crotch, only the thin silk of her panties separating his finger from her hot, wet slit.

"Oh . . . yeah. . . ." Her words came out in little whimpers, then she moaned as he stroked again. She clutched his shirt and dragged him closer, then devoured his lips, thrusting her tongue deep into his mouth.

His hand slid inside her panties and he cupped her hot mound. She quivered all over at the feel of his big, masculine hand covering her so intimately.

"Take me," she gasped against his ear. "Now. Here. Against the door."

She shoved her panties down and kicked them off, then gazed at him with desperate longing.

His hands fumbled at his belt and his jeans hit the floor with a *clunk,* then she felt his hot, iron-hard rod brush across her hip, then spear between her thighs, stroking along her slit. She tightened her legs, embracing his cock as it glided back and forth over her slippery flesh.

She felt so wickedly sexy. Wildly wanton. She ripped open her blouse, heedless of buttons tugging free of the buttonholes, a few flying off and bouncing across the wooden floor. She tucked the fabric of her bra cups under her breasts, baring them while leaving them framed by her aqua lace bra.

He smiled and leaned forward to capture one puckered nipple in his mouth, then he sucked and she moaned loudly at the exquisite sensation.

"Inside me. I want you to—"

"What do you want me to do, Hanna?"

He sucked her other nipple deep into his mouth as he watched her face.

"I want you to . . . to . . ." She hesitated, wanting him desperately, but not sure how to put it into words.

His tongue flicked her hard nipple, then he sucked deep and hard.

"Tell me, honey." He pushed his pelvis tight against her, pressing her against the door. His cock, so rigid and hot, pressed against her needy flesh. Oh, heavens, but she needed him inside her.

He nuzzled her ear. "Be dirty," he coaxed. "Say it."

His finger toyed with her nipple, and his cock twitched between her legs.

"Fuck me." The coarse words escaped her mouth, followed by a gasp of pleasure as his pelvis pivoted upward and he pressed closer, putting pressure on her clit.

He kissed her cheek, then smiled. His eyebrow quirked up.

He eased the pressure of his pelvis against her, then pushed forward again. His pelvis pressed her against the door, his cock still embedded between her thighs, pressed against her hot, needy flesh.

"So you want me to . . ." He rocked his hips, stimulating her clit in waves. ". . . fuck you?"

"Oh, yeah." Her knees weakened and she clung to his broad, strong shoulders. "Fuck me. Fuck me now."

His fingers stroked down her belly, then his fingertip brushed her clit. She wailed at the intense pleasure.

He grasped his cock and nudged the head against her. He pushed into her slick flesh and buried his cock head inside her.

Breathing became difficult as pleasure swept through her. He grasped her legs and lifted. She wrapped them around him. His long cock plunged into her.

"Oh, yes." Hanna clung to J.M.

Hot and iron-hard, his cock filled her like nothing else could. She squeezed him, trying to hold him inside her, draw him deeper into her body.

He drew back, then thrust forward again.

"Oh, yes," she whimpered. "Oh, God." She gasped, sucking in air. It felt so good. She felt so wild. The pleasure swept over her, building . . . building. . . .

"Yeah, honey," he said as he plunged forward, his face fierce with passion. With every thrust he thumped her against the door. She sucked in air . . . faster and deeper. Matching his thrusts.

She felt so sexy . . . so wanton. . . .

Bliss washed over her, the crest of the orgasm rolling closer.

Banging. Knocking? Someone was knocking on the door.

Oh, God, whoever it was would figure out what they were doing and—

Her breath caught as the thought pierced her awareness, then she moaned as a wild pulse of pleasure gripped her.

J.M. thrust faster and harder.

The knocking stopped.

She clung to J.M., her legs wrapped tightly around him. He groaned and flooded her insides with heat. She wailed as her pleasure erupted with more force.

He rode her as her orgasm went on and on, enhanced by the knowledge that someone stood outside the door, hearing them, knowing what they were doing. She gasped again and moaned, riding the intense ecstasy as it exploded through every part of her. Then she collapsed against the door, gasping for breath.

"Oh, my God. That was incredible."

J.M. smiled at her.

"I do believe you have a bit of a wild side, Miss Lane."

She felt the heat of a blush color her cheeks as she realized she'd wantonly been fucked by a man against his front door, while someone stood on the other side listening. And that's what had triggered her orgasm.

Grey stared at the door. The sounds from the other side were unmistakable. He grinned. Jeremy was banging some woman against the door. And judging from her wild moans, she was enjoying it immensely.

Grey had to drag himself away, enthralled by her wails of bliss, remembering Hanna as she had cried out in orgasm last night.

Grey turned around and returned to his car, parked on the street in front of the house. He slumped into the driver's seat and set the bottle of wine on the seat next to him. He'd brought the wine as a gift to thank Jeremy for helping him with Hanna's problem. He wanted to tell Jeremy about their success last night.

Grey rubbed his hand over the back of his neck. Last night had been a great start, but would it continue? Would he be able to make her come like that all the time? Every time? The fact that her orgasm was strictly a result of a hypnotic trance made him feel very uncertain. He hadn't actually made her come. Words and images from her own mind had done that. When it came down to just the two of them, would it really work?

He glanced at the house. Bushes covered with dark pink flowers bloomed out front and the rambling garden was full of plants of different-colored foliage, from yellow-green to dark red. Flowers of rich red, purple, and blue abounded.

He felt a little jealous of Jeremy and the woman behind the door. For their easy sexuality. Their ability to just fall into the moment and have great sex.

A movement at the window drew his attention. The blinds were open and he could see the vague shapes of two figures sitting on the couch. Grey pushed himself up in the seat. As he fumbled in his pocket for his car keys, he realized Jeremy's guest was a woman with long blond hair. A lot like Hanna's.

J.M. held Hanna's hand as she fidgeted on the couch beside him.

"I wanted to let you know that I saw my ex-boyfriend last night and . . ."

At her hesitation, he prompted, "Did you make love with him?"

She nodded.

"And did it work?"

Again she nodded, looking a little guilty.

He ignored the trails of jealousy threading their way through him and slid his arm around her.

"It's okay. In fact, it's great. You need to know you can orgasm whenever you want."

"I know." She drew her hand from his grasp and fiddled with her fingers. "There's something else. He and I talked and . . ." She hesitated. "He told me he loves me."

J.M.'s gut clenched. He didn't want to lose Hanna. She'd brought a special light to his life.

"And how do you feel about him?"

She stared at J.M. with shimmering blue eyes.

"I love him. I always have."

"I see." So it was over between them.

"But, J.M." She took his hands. "I love you, too."

J.M.'s breath locked in his lungs. Love?

A knock sounded at the door. Actually, more like a pounding.

Hanna released his hands and he strolled to the door, then drew it open.

His student Grey Bennet stood in the doorway, breathing hard, his face drawn tight in anger.

"Grey, what is it?" J.M. asked.

A choked sound from Hanna surprised him, but he didn't shift his gaze from the emotional man in front of him.

"What the hell is going on here?" Grey's heart pounded as he strode into the house, pushing past J.M. The moment Grey saw Hanna sitting on the couch wearing only a man's shirt, her eyes wide in shock as she stared at him, his chest clenched so tight he thought he'd collapse from the pain.

"What the hell are you doing here with him?" His arm thrust out as he pointed at Jeremy.

"I . . ." She toyed with the top button of the shirt. *His* shirt. "You knew I was seeing someone else."

"But after last night, after everything I told you." His fists clenched tightly at his sides. "God damn it, Hanna. How could you have sex with another man?"

The sounds he'd heard behind the door echoed through his head with alarming clarity. She'd come, long and hard . . . with Jeremy. Well, of course she would. How the hell could Grey compete with a man like that? A sexual master?

God damn it. He'd lost her for sure. He felt so helpless.

She was pushing herself to her feet, saying something, but he couldn't hear her over the thumping of his heart.

It became difficult to breathe. He turned around and strode from the house.

Hanna watched Grey climb into his car and drive away. Guilt bombarded her. She sucked in a lungful of air and tried to calm her breathing.

Numbness crept through her as she pulled on her denim skirt and tied the shirt at her waist, then tucked her undergarments and blouse into her purse.

As she reached for the doorknob, she turned to J.M. "How do you know Grey?"

He sighed. "I teach the Kama Sutra course."

Some part of her knew she should react to that, knew she should feel some emotion, but she couldn't even begin to identify what.

She pulled open the door and stepped into the bright sunlight.

thirteen

Hanna rode her bike along the path that followed the river, the wind whooshing past her ears. The light glittering on the water as the sun settled low on the horizon, the birds singing in the trees, and the squirrels dancing along tree branches did nothing to calm her roiling emotions.

The look on Grey's face when he'd seen her in J.M.'s living room wearing only J.M.'s shirt still haunted her.

How could you have sex with another man?

Grey's words still rang through her head.

An image of his face—of the pain lacing his features—cut through her soul. It had been a big step for him to tell her he loved her. Then for her to make love to another man . . . the very next day.

She had been a fool.

She had to make it up to Grey. Let him know how much she loved him.

But what about J.M.? What did he mean to her?

J.M.

Damn it, that was a whole different disaster.

She finally let the fact that kept churning through her brain rise to the surface.

J.M. is not a student in the Kama Sutra course. He's the instructor!

She'd been terrified at the thought of being one of thirty students in Jeremy Smith's course and she'd wound up being a student of one—with very personal tutoring.

Was it possible Grace had orchestrated the whole thing? Suggested he date Hanna so he could help her with her *problem*?

Hanna realized she was probably just being paranoid, but then Grace was pretty protective of Hanna and probably wouldn't think anything of suggesting he might find her interesting, maybe even mentioning she worked at the café across the street. If Grace told him about Hanna's problem, his natural desire to help—he was a very caring man—might have led him to take pity on her.

Oh, God, had Grace arranged for him to come to the Hot Spot Café after suggesting Hanna have sex with a stranger in hopes that . . . Her cheeks flushed hotter as she remembered how she had stripped off her clothes in front of him. And he'd encouraged her.

Of course, what guy wouldn't encourage a woman in a situation like that?

Hanna rode for over an hour, the same thoughts tumbling through her mind over and over again. Finally, she stopped at a little restaurant for a salad and something cold to drink.

What she couldn't figure out was why J.M.—Jeremy—had helped Grey. That just seemed strange. Unless Jeremy hadn't known Grey was Hanna's ex-boyfriend.

By the time she got home, it was after 10:00 P.M. She ignored the flashing light on her answering machine. After a nice warm shower, she flopped into bed and fell asleep immediately.

The next morning, she made herself some coffee and eggs. Once she'd finished the last bite of her meal, she pushed aside her plate and dialed the phone.

"Hello?"

"Hi, Amy. It's Hanna. You told me you'd like some full-time work this summer if possible."

Amy's voice perked up. "Yeah. That would be great."

"Super. I was thinking about a week. I'm going out of town. Are you available to start this afternoon?"

Hanna knocked on the apartment door, wondering if she had been too impulsive. Maybe she should have called ahead before taking the two-hour bus trip to New York.

The door opened and Grey stared at her in surprise.

"Hanna? What are you doing here?" He didn't smile, but his eyes glittered with subdued emotion.

"I think we should talk."

"Okay."

He picked up her suitcase and carried it inside.

She followed him, closing the door behind her.

"Nice place," she said as she glanced around. She knew his company had provided him with a one-bedroom apartment for the duration of his contract here.

Grey placed her suitcase at the end of the couch. Not in the bedroom. Was that because he didn't want to assume too much or because he didn't want her to stay?

"Why don't you sit down?" he suggested, gesturing toward the couch. "Do you want something?"

"Some lemonade or a glass of water would be great."

He went into the kitchen and returned a moment later with two tall glasses of lemonade. He handed her one, then sat down beside her. She took a sip of her icy drink, then placed it on the coffee table in front of her.

"Grey, I'm really sorry I hurt you by . . . when I was with J.M."

His mouth formed a grim line and his green eyes turned cool.

She took his hand, holding it between hers. He did not pull away. A good sign.

"Grey, you've got to remember that I was already dating J.M. . . . already *sleeping* with J.M. I know you don't want to hear that, but you and I had broken up."

"But I told you I loved you. Didn't that make any difference?"

"Of course it made a difference, but I was confused and uncertain. You and I went out for over a year. If you loved me, why didn't you tell me before?"

Grey drew back, clearly uncomfortable with the direction of the conversation.

He took a deep breath, then sat in silence for a moment, obviously struggling to come up with words. "I've been keeping a secret from you."

A dizzying sense of apprehension streamed through her. She flattened her hand on the couch cushion to steady herself.

"I should have told you sooner," he continued. He took her hands in his and gazed at her, his eyes imploring. "But I was just so afraid of losing you."

The hairs on the back of her neck quivered to attention.

"What is it?"

His gaze dropped to their joined hands. "When I was a child I had an illness that left me sterile. If you stay with me, we'll never have children, none of our own, anyway—none that are yours and mine."

"Oh." What could she say? When she and Grey were together and she'd fallen in love with him, she had hoped they would eventually get married and have kids. Those hopes had arisen again since he told her he loved her, despite her confusion about why he'd said it. Despite her relationship with J.M.

Because, deep down, she knew it was Grey she really loved.

"I knew when I told you about it," he continued, "that I would lose you."

Her head shook back and forth of its own accord.

"Grey, I—"

"No, don't say anything. I know how big this is. It's taken me years to get used to the idea I'll never be a father. I don't want you giving me false hope when we both know you need time to come to grips with this."

"You're right. I will need some time." She reached up and stroked his cheeks. "But I don't need time to decide that I still love you." She twined her fingers in his sandy brown hair, then leaned toward him. "And I will always love you."

She kissed him, gently caressing his lips with hers, then she stroked his lips with her tongue. His arms slid around her and he pulled her tight to his body.

Even though pain and trepidation pummeled his insides, Grey felt a great sense of relief at having revealed something that had eaten away at him for the past year. Now Hanna knew. She would make her decision. One way or another, he could get on with his life.

As he felt her lips moving under his, her soft, warm body pressed against him, he felt a rising hope that she might decide to stay with him, even if it meant having a family through nontraditional means.

She took his hand and pulled it to her breast as her tongue slipped into his mouth. The feel of her soft, round flesh under his fingers, the tightened nipple pressing into his palm, sent his pulse racing.

She began to unbutton her blouse and he froze. She wanted to make love and so did he, but apprehension consumed him. If they made love, he had to bring her to orgasm. And he only knew one proven way to do that.

"Honey, I want to make love to you, but can we do the hypnosis again?"

Hanna noticed Grey's pale face. She was confident she could reach orgasm in his arms, but she knew he was so intimidated by J.M.'s prowess he didn't believe it.

"Of course. That would be great."

The hypnosis would definitely work and it would be a great distraction. In fact, the memory of the leather-clad biker holding her tight against his body, gliding his long, hard cock into her as they rode along the highway, filled her with heat.

She rested her hands on Grey's shoulders and leaned toward him, aware of the heat of him so close.

"This time, when we do a fantasy," she murmured into his ear, her breasts feeling heavy, "I want you in the starring role." She nuzzled his raspy cheek, then kissed the corner of his mouth. "And I know I'll have an absolutely mind-blowing orgasm."

That would certainly give him some level of confidence in his sexual prowess. And she could hardly wait to have Grey plunder her body in what would absolutely be a heart-thudding, intensely erotic lovemaking session.

Grey licked his lips as he watched Hanna lying on his couch, totally naked. The voice on the tape ended. Hanna's chest rose and fell in a steady, even rhythm.

He walked through the same script he'd used last time to lower her barriers and find a sexual fantasy she would like to experience.

"Remember, you are safe and loved," he said. "I will not judge. I will find your fantasy just as exciting and arousing as you do."

He wondered what fantasy she would come up with this time.

"I'm going to touch you on the shoulder in a moment. When I do, lift your head, open your eyes, and tell me in a clear, loud voice what your sexual fantasy is."

"Pirates," she said.

"You want me to be a pirate and kidnap you?"

"More than one pirate," she responded.

More? She wanted a ménage à trois?

"Two pirates?" he asked in surprise.

"Four."

His cock bulged painfully.

"Okay, now relax." If only his cock would listen to that directive. "Go deeper into the trance. Relax your mind and body and sink down deeper and deeper."

He shifted in his chair, seeking his own comfortable

position. Which was pretty hard, given his cramped, throbbing cock.

"It is a dark night and there's a full moon illuminating the sandy beach around you. The white light glitters on the calm ocean beyond. Beside you, there are trees and bushes casting shadows on the sand. You are sitting on a large rock, feeling the cold stone against your hot pussy. I am standing behind you, a pirate captain who kidnapped you from your home and brought you here. You hear rustling and see three pirates step out of the shadows."

Hanna shifted on the rock. The rough, cold stone rubbed against her throbbing, needy pussy. Three figures stepped out of the shadows and approached her. A shiver of apprehension raced down her spine.

"They are tall and broad and menacing-looking. They stand in front of you, in a half circle, staring at you. I pull you against me and tear open your blouse, exposing your naked breasts."

The cool night air danced against her naked flesh and her nipples hardened. She could feel their gazes raking over her breasts. Her breathing increased.

"You are frightened, even though you know deep down inside you are safe. I sense your fear and don't want you to run away, so I grasp your arms, keeping you pinned to the rock."

Pirate Grey grasped her arms and held them tight.

"The other pirates unbutton their pants and pull out their long, hard cocks. You stare at them and know they are going to thrust those hard cocks inside you soon. Your fear turns to wild excitement, but you can't let them know that. Each one looks quite different, but all are quite handsome."

Each of them was muscular and broad shouldered. The leftmost man, who stood about six one, wore a bandanna around his head, and his dark, feral eyes glinted. He tugged out a long, thick, very hard cock. The next man was a little shorter, with a square jaw, shoulder-length dark blond hair, and a wicked smile. His cock was also long, but with a broader head. Whiskers shadowed the third man's face, and his smooth, muscular chest was bare under his black leather vest. He had the biggest cock of all, which he stroked with pride.

"The one to your right moves forward and strokes your breasts."

Her gaze stayed on his long cock as he stepped forward. He stroked her breasts and the nipples lengthened under his rough fingertips.

"The middle one steps forward and pulls up your skirt, then tears off your panties."

She gasped as he exposed her wet pussy.

"All three of them stare at your pussy and you get wetter."

She could feel it dripping. She longed for one of them—all of them—to touch her pussy. To stroke her and make her come.

"One of them pulls the skirt over your head and tosses

it aside. They stroke their cocks and stand in front of you. You feel a deep desire to take them in your mouth."

She licked her lips, wanting to touch those cocks. Wanting to lick them. Her lips tingled with the need to wrap around one of those delicious-looking cocks and start sucking.

"One wraps his hand around your head and pulls it toward his cock, touching his cock head against your lips."

His hard cock pressed against her lips.

"You open and he plunges it inside your mouth. At first, you are overwhelmed, but then you lick the tip of him, then circle your tongue around the crown."

She loved having this hard cock in her mouth. The head filled her mouth and she licked it, swirling her tongue around the crown.

"You suck him deep into your mouth, then down your throat, having no problem taking him. It's exciting having his hard cock in your mouth."

She'd never taken a man so deep, and she loved it.

"You suck and lick and he grunts, then comes in your mouth."

She felt hot liquid erupt in her mouth.

"You love it. It feels so good, and his cum tastes wonderful as you swallow it down. He pulls free and the next man thrusts his cock into your mouth."

Grey rubbed his own cock, wishing it were in her mouth. Her tongue slipped out of her mouth and circled her lips.

"You suck and pulse your mouth around him, then take him deep into your throat. He fucks your mouth, sliding in and out, and you keep up easily. Sucking him. Teasing him. He grasps your head and holds it tight against him. You suck and suck until he erupts inside you. You swallow his tasty cum, too. Finally, the third man fucks your mouth and you suck him to climax."

Grey watched her, her nipples hard and thrusting upward. Her legs were splayed wantonly, her pussy visibly wet. What should he do now? Was it possible she wanted more than to suck cock for these men?

"You lie back on the rock, wondering what they are going to do next. Although this fantasy is very real to you, I want part of you to know that this is a scene we're playing out. If anything happens that you don't want to happen, say the word 'cat' as loud as you can so I know there's a problem."

He should have done that sooner, but he had forgotten. They hadn't planned on this fantasy tonight.

"Although you've just satisfied all of these men, they still look hungry for you. Impossible as it seems, their cocks are still hard and sticking out. I stroke your breasts as one of them steps forward and presses his cock to your slit."

Her legs opened wider, as if in anticipation. Grey longed to cup her breasts in his hands and stroke, then to lean over and grasp one hard, hot nipple in his mouth and suck.

"He thrusts forward and pumps into you hard and fast."

Hanna's breathing accelerated as the glorious cock pushed inside her. She squeezed it, feeling its long, hard length. Pleasure built in her in waves. The cock thrust deep inside her. Grey's hands stroked her breasts.

"It feels wonderful having his hard cock glide in and out of you and the pleasure builds, but you hold off that orgasm."

But it quivered through her. She wanted it. She needed it.

"Knowing you can have it anytime you want it, but choosing to delay. He grunts and comes inside you, then pulls out."

She chose to delay. Knowing it would be better.

"The next man steps forward and shoves his big cock inside you. You moan at the pleasure."

Yes, a second big cock sliding inside her.

"He fucks you hard and fast, filling you with his cum in no time."

Pleasure washed over her. An orgasm so close she could barely contain it.

"The third man steps up and thrusts his cock inside you. It goes deeper than the other two and stimulates you even more."

She arched and clenched him tight inside her. She wanted him to ride her, hard and fast, thrusting her to a blazing orgasm.

"It feels incredibly erotic having him thrusting inside you, fucking you after the two others fucked you. After you sucked all their cocks. He erupts inside you and, as he pulls out, you feel their cum dripping down your thighs."

Drops of warm stickiness trailed down her thighs. She knew it was their cum.

Grey watched Hanna's breasts heave up and down with her heavy breathing. He wanted to kneel down beside her and stroke her breasts, then suck them into his mouth. He wanted to climb on top of her and sink his cock into her soft, wet pussy.

He could awaken her. Or keep her in the trance but tell her to fuck him.

Or he could give her more intense pleasure as she continued her fantasy.

"The first man pulls you to your feet and he drives his cock into you again. He lifts your legs and wraps them around him. A moment later, you feel something nudge against your ass and you realize it's a cock."

Grey paused, waiting to see if she'd say the safe word. Instead, she lay there expectantly, her breasts heaving. Wow, he never would have believed Hanna would have such wildly erotic fantasies.

Hanna clung to the big, sexy pirate, tightening her vagina around his long, hard cock. The other cock pressed tightly against her ass, nuzzling her opening. She clenched in anticipation, worried about that long, wide cock pushing into her.

"The other man's cock pushes against your opening, then he slides inside a little. You open easily to him, with no pain or discomfort. In fact, it is intensely pleasurable."

She moaned at the erotic sensation of a cock pushing into her ass. She never knew it would feel so incredible.

"He pushes forward and fills you. You have two cocks inside you, filling you, giving you pleasure."

"Oh, yes," she moaned, clinging to her pirate while the other one impaled her from behind.

fourteen

Grey could imagine her standing sandwiched between the two men. His cock throbbed in need.

"They start to move. Their cocks glide within you. You can't believe how intensely pleasurable it is."

He couldn't believe how intensely erotic it was. She seemed restless again, but she didn't say the word. Maybe she just wanted more freedom of movement.

"You can move a little if you want to, but stay lying on the couch."

Her left hand, which sat near the couch back, opened and closed.

"Tell me what you want."

"Cock," she said.

Of course. The other man.

"The third pirate moves toward you and you grasp his cock in your hand and stroke it. He moans. Now you have all three cocks under your control as the men fuck you."

Her other hand started to open and close in the same manner as the first had.

Grey realized there were four men present and he was one of them.

"Do you want my cock?" he asked.

She nodded.

"Okay, I step toward you and you grasp my cock. You stroke it in your hand. Now you have four cocks."

His cock longed to be in her hand. In her pussy. *God, in her ass.*

Her hand still quivered as it clamped open and closed.

"Tell me what you want."

"Your cock. Here."

He hesitated. Uncertain.

"Here," she insisted.

He stood up and moved toward her, then knelt beside her. Her hand grasped wildly in the air. He wrapped his hand around her wrist and she calmed.

He unzipped his fly and released his cock, then guided her hand to his flesh. She wrapped her fingers around him and stroked. He couldn't believe how incredibly intense the sensations were.

"You are . . ." His voice crumpled. He cleared his throat, trying to keep his head as she stroked him with her hand. "The men are thrusting into you. You know they're going to come soon."

And he would, too, if she kept doing that.

"They groan and both the cocks erupt inside you. You can feel their cum inside you."

She moaned. Damn, he didn't want her to come yet. He wanted her to come while he was inside her.

"You don't orgasm. You're so close, but you choose not to orgasm yet. You want to wait. For me. You want me inside you."

He stilled her hand, knowing he would erupt any second with her continued movements.

"You stop caressing the two cocks in your hands. The two men pull out of you and . . ."

The need for her pulsed through him, too intense to ignore.

"I'm going to count to three in a moment. On the count of three, you're going to open your eyes, then you're going to sit up and grab my cock, then start sucking it. You'll stroke my balls and bring me close to coming, but will stop before I do. When I calm down, you'll suck again, bringing me close again. Then you'll stop and lay back on the couch and ask me—in as sexy a way as you can think of—to fuck you. Then we'll make love and it will be fantastic and exciting and intensely pleasurable. You will be intensely turned on and as soon as you feel me come inside you, you'll experience an intense orgasm.

"One. Two. Three!"

She opened her eyes and sat up. She smiled and

grabbed his cock. He almost fell over as he felt her lips surround him, then his cock slide into her hot, wet mouth. She sucked the cock head and ran her tongue around the edge, then she sucked him deep into her mouth. Deeper than she ever had before. She opened her throat and took him all the way in. She fondled his balls as she sucked his hard cock.

Oh, God, it felt so hot and so good. He felt like he was going to . . .

She pulled away, leaving his cock exposed to the cool air. She continued to stroke his balls and he closed his eyes, enjoying the play of her hands on him. Then her mouth covered him again. She stroked and sucked, bringing him close to the edge again, then she released him.

She smiled, then lay back on the couch, opening her legs to him. She stroked her fingers over her nipples.

"Your pirate cock is so big and hard. I want you inside me so badly." She stared at his cock hungrily, licking her lips.

"I want you to shove your huge cock inside me and fuck me. Hard and fast. Pound into me until I scream in ecstasy."

His cock twitched.

He climbed over her and pressed his cock head to her slit. It was incredibly hot and wet. He pushed forward and impaled her in one hard, long thrust. She conformed to his shape, her pussy gripping him tightly. He drew back and thrust again. She clutched him close to her.

"Oh, God, that feels so good," she murmured against his ear.

He thrust faster and harder, pounding into her as she'd requested. Her little gasps turned to moans, and then to wails of pleasure. His balls tightened and then he erupted inside her. Right on cue she gasped, then moaned in pleasure, clearly reaching orgasm. He pumped and pumped. Her cries increased until she screamed in ecstasy.

Her orgasm seemed to go on forever as he happily thrust, riding her through her pleasure. Finally, her shrieks subsided and she clung to him, her face pushed up tight against his chest.

An idea occurred to him.

"Now, you'll have another orgasm. Maybe more."

He thrust, then swirled, then thrust. She clung tighter and wailed louder, her vagina tightening around his cock, gripping it tightly as he thrust and thrust. A second orgasm, then a third, tore through her. He pumped, deep and hard, as she reached her bliss a fourth time.

Finally, she slumped in his arms, clinging tightly to him. He held her close against him, savoring the feel of her naked body against his. This was surely heaven.

Finally, he smiled down at her . . . and realized her eyes were glassy. She was still in a trance. She'd made love to a pirate in a fantasy. Not to him.

Hanna rolled onto her back and stretched, the soft white cotton sheets caressing her limbs. She rolled over the other way to see an empty pillow beside her. A vague memory of Grey giving her a tender kiss good-bye before he left for work this morning washed through her brain.

She smiled. Last night had been phenomenal. Images of the hard, male bodies made her body flush with excitement. Heat melted through her at the memory of the rough men using her for their pleasure, of sliding their cocks into her mouth, of those cocks pounding into her body. Need spiked through her and her fingers stroked her hot, dampening slit as she remembered first one pirate entering her vagina, then another pushing into her from behind.

She closed her eyes and imagined the one in front was Grey thrusting forward. The one behind her kissing her cheek as he burrowed into her was J.M.

Excitement blazed through her and her fingers found her clit, then vibrated on it. In her fantasy, the men kissed her while thrusting . . . sandwiching her between two walls of hard, muscular, male chests . . . two long, hard cocks driving into her.

Her finger worked faster as a swell of scorching pleasure tore through her, sending her wailing over the edge.

She flopped back, gasping for air. That was the fastest, easiest orgasm she'd ever experienced. Her cheeks burned at the thought that her fantasy of anonymous men had turned into two very real men—Grey and J.M.—making love to her at the same time. Did she really want that?

Oh, yeah. Absolutely.

The definite certainty startled her. Oh, God, what was happening to her? What would people think if they knew about her wild fantasies?

At that moment, she realized she worried too damn much about how others might judge her. Why should she care about what other people thought of her desires . . . or actions for that matter?

In matters of sex, the only people who mattered were her and her lover. Or lovers. What they did was private and it didn't affect anyone else—so why shouldn't she act a little wild?

As she stared at the ceiling, she sucked in a deep breath. Letting herself loose and embracing her secret fantasies had helped her tap into something very powerful—and deeply sexual—within her.

She remembered how fantastic the sex had been between her and Grey when he'd turned the fantasy into the real thing. Getting in touch with her sexuality was good for her—and it was good for Grey. After last night, she didn't think Grey would judge her badly for her desires. And she knew J.M. wouldn't.

Hanna stared out the window of Grey's tenth-story apartment at the bright sunshine glittering off the windows of the buildings beyond. She thought about what Grey had told her last evening, that he couldn't have kids.

Over the day, she thought long and hard about the issue. Of course she wanted to have kids. And there was nothing she'd like more than a little boy or girl that was part her, part Grey. But no matter how much she rolled the ideas around in her head, she realized that life without Grey would be worse than giving up on the dream. The thought of being without him triggered an emptiness deep inside her. She loved Grey and she wanted him in her life.

That evening, she cooked him a great dinner of chicken parmesan and fresh-baked rolls. One of his favorite meals. She set the table with candles and wineglasses and they smiled and chatted over dinner. Nothing serious.

At the end of the meal, they cleared away the plates and sat together on the couch.

"Grey, I have something to say to you."

Grey placed his wineglass on the table and turned to her, his heart sinking.

The time had come. Hanna would now tell him she loved him but had to leave him anyway.

His heart ached.

"I've had time to think today," she continued. "About you and me. About the fact you can't have children. And it's not important to me."

His eyebrows furrowed downward. He couldn't be hearing her right.

She rested her hand on his.

"At least, not as important as you are."

Warmth rippled through him.

"I love you," she continued, "and together, we'll figure it out. We can be happy, just the two of us. If we decide we really want to have kids, we can adopt. Or maybe use artificial insemination. We have options." She stroked his cheek. "The only option that is unacceptable to me is not having you in my life."

His heart soared and he drew her into his arms, squeezing her tightly.

"Hanna, I love you so much. I can't believe you've decided—"

A loud knock sounded at the door. Reluctantly, he drew back from her. Who the hell was that?

"I'll get it." Hanna gave him a warm smile as she stood up, then went to answer the door.

J.M. stood outside the apartment door. He had slipped into the lobby by following another person, concerned Grey would not let him in.

He wanted to set things straight with Grey. J.M. liked the man and respected how dedicated he was to his woman. It was too bad the woman Grey loved was also the woman J.M. had come to care for so deeply.

J.M. rapped on the door again and waited. A second later, the doorknob turned and Hanna peered out the chained opening.

"J.M.?" She unchained the door and pulled it open. "What are you doing here?"

"I came to talk to Grey."

Grey appeared behind Hanna and rested his arm around her shoulder in a protective, territorial gesture.

"Grey, I didn't know you were Hanna's boyfriend. And I sincerely wanted to help you."

Hanna turned her head and gazed at Grey. He stepped away, but his scowl remained.

"Come in," Hanna said.

J.M. followed her into the apartment living room. Grey disappeared through a door, probably into the kitchen. The aroma of chicken and the sound of plates clacking together on the other side of the door probably meant Hanna and Grey had just finished dinner and Grey was doing the dishes.

"Would you like a drink?" Hanna asked.

J.M. noticed a bottle of white wine on the table with two partially full glasses.

"Wine would be great."

She grabbed a stemmed glass from a cupboard beside the dining table, filled it, then handed it to him. J.M. sat down in an armchair and Hanna settled on the couch.

"I think he needs a few minutes," Hanna said.

Of course he would. J.M. had just invaded Grey's space. And he must be hating the thought of seeing Hanna and J.M. together.

"Hanna, I'm sorry things worked out this way."

She nodded. "I . . . just want to ask you one thing."

"What is it?"

"Did you start dating me because of my sister?"

"Your sister?" Confusion darted through him.

"Grace Jones."

Hanna is Grace's sister?

"I didn't know Grace is your sister. Why would you think . . . ?"

He remembered Grace telling him her sister was going to take his course, then suggesting he date her. He had forgotten all about that.

Hanna raised her eyebrows.

"No, it's nothing. Your sister, she just worries about you."

"She did suggest you date me, didn't she?" Her words were accusing.

"Yes, but I didn't take her seriously. And believe me—"

"Did she tell you about my problem?"

"Yes, but—"

"Are you telling me you didn't figure it out when we, when I couldn't . . ."

"Hanna, a lot of women have that problem. I didn't make the link between that and Grace's sister."

She seemed to relax a little. "So that night in the café, Grace didn't send you."

J.M. took Hanna's hands. "Hanna, I made love to you because I was attracted to you. And the more I got to know you, the more I came to care for you. It had nothing to do with your sister."

Grey opened the kitchen door and noticed Jeremy holding hands with Hanna. When Grey heard Jeremy tell her he cared for her, Grey closed the door again, blocking out the disturbing scene.

Damn it, the man had come to win Hanna back. Well, Grey wouldn't let her go without a fight.

fifteen

"Grey?" Hanna peered into the kitchen and saw Grey wiping the counter beside the sink. The dishes were all put away, the stove shone, and the room was neat and tidy.

She stepped into the room and closed the door behind her.

"J.M. was going to find a hotel."

Grey stared at her, and the sharp look in his eyes told her he knew what she was going to ask and he wouldn't be happy with her request.

"I . . . uh . . . suggested he could stay here."

"Why in hell did you do that?"

She walked toward him and placed her hand on his arm. Tension emanated from him.

"I really think you two should talk. He really did want to help you."

"Hanna, surely you can understand why I don't want him here."

She sighed. "Please don't feel threatened by him." She moved in closer, curling her hands around Grey's neck and kissing his jawline. "It's *you* I'm in love with."

He scowled, but his hands went around her waist and he drew her in close to his body.

"Fine. But I'm going straight to bed." He nuzzled her ear and tingles danced down her spine. "And I'm hoping you're coming with me."

Grey shoved the kitchen door open and strode through the living room to the linen cupboard in the hall, then grabbed a couple of pillows and a blanket and tossed them onto the couch.

"I don't have a spare room, so you can bunk there. I'm hitting the sack," he said to J.M.

Grey turned and disappeared into the bedroom, but not before sending Hanna a meaningful stare. The door thumped closed behind him.

"Hanna, I don't want to cause any problems. Maybe I should just go to a hotel."

"No, it's okay. I'm hoping the three of us can talk tomorrow."

She hoped the two men would clear the air between them. She felt that Grey had enjoyed having another man to confide in. Not that that could really continue now, which was too bad.

"Make yourself comfortable," Hanna said. "I'll see you in the morning."

Hanna pulled on her nightgown and slipped into bed beside Grey. He had been reading his book ever since she'd entered the room, never looking up.

She snuggled in beside him.

He lowered his book. The glower she expected to see on his face was not there. Instead, she saw vulnerability and pain.

She rested her hand on his shoulder. "Grey, what is it?" She stroked his arm, encouraging him to go on.

He sucked in a breath. "I know I can't give you what he can."

"Grey, I already told you. The fact you can't have children—"

"No, I mean sexually."

She smiled warmly.

"Sweetheart, you've given me just as much as he has."

"No, I haven't, Hanna. Every time you've come with me, you were in a trance. It wasn't real."

She grinned. "It felt real to me."

"But it wasn't me who triggered them. It was fantasy men."

The vulnerability in his eyes tore at her heart.

"Oh, my God, Grey. No. It was you. It was your words. It was your images. You were the one who made me come. Again and again."

She slid her fingers under one strap of her silky night-gown and dropped it over her shoulder, then did the same with the other.

"If you don't believe me, I'll just have to prove it."

She took his hand and slid it under her nightgown to cup her breast. Her nipple puckered and pushed into his palm.

"I don't know." His head jerked toward the door. "With him out there, we'll have to hold back."

She shimmied and the nightgown dropped downward, baring her breasts. One totally naked, the other covered by his strong, masculine hand. She saw his cock stiffen under the thin sheets.

"I'm tired of holding back," she said with a wicked grin.

She stroked her bare breast with her fingers. His moss green eyes darkened with desire. She smiled seductively as she pushed her nightgown down her hips to her knees, then she rolled onto her seat and flicked the silky garment to the floor.

She pushed the sheet down. His erection strained at his pajama bottoms. She tucked her fingers under the elastic waistband, then rolled them downward. He shoved them off his feet, letting them drop to the floor, then stripped off the top. She sat on his thighs, her back to him, and pulled his hands to her breasts. He sat up as he cupped them and stroked. Electricity danced along her spine as he kissed her neck, right at the base.

She leaned back against him and reveled in the delicious sensations of his hands moving over her breasts . . . his lips caressing her neck. His fingers caressed down her stomach and stroked lightly over her clitoris, then across her inner thigh.

She eased him back to a reclining position, then shifted onto her knees and leaned forward, taking his growing cock between her lips, teasing the tip with her tongue. His hands slipped to her hips and he drew her toward him. When his mouth covered her molten slit, she moaned. He licked her as she sucked his cock deeper into her mouth.

His tongue pulsed into her and she dove down on him, swallowing him entirely. She bobbed up and down . . . up and down. His tongue circled her clit in erotic spirals.

He stopped to lick his fingers, then teased her nipple with warm, damp fingertips.

"I didn't know you liked bikers," he said in a low, rumbling voice. "And pirates."

At the memory of Grey dressed in black leather, fucking her from behind, heat scorched through her.

His mouth covered her again and his tongue gently jabbed her clit, and he sucked. It was too much. She flew over the edge, moaning around his cock as the orgasm claimed her.

He stroked her breast with one hand, then drew his still erect cock from her mouth, his tongue still thrusting against her clitoris. She moaned. He sucked and teased her, extending her pleasure with a pulsing, erotic rhythm.

Finally, she sighed and collapsed on him, then rolled sideways. He crawled down the bed and flopped down beside her, smiling broadly.

"That was you, not a hypnotic fantasy," she said, concerned he'd think she was fantasizing about someone else.

"Prove it."

He grinned and climbed over her, then pressed his hot cock against her wet opening and slid into her. She sighed at the exquisite feel of his steel-hard cock gliding into her.

"Oh, yes." She stroked his cheek. "Make love to me, Grey. Make me come."

He slowly thrust in, then out.

"Yes," she moaned.

In, then out. Deeper.

"Yes."

He thrust faster. Deeper. Harder.

"Oh, God, yes."

Intense pleasure swept through her. Rising. Swelling. She ached with the need to reach that pinnacle as she wrapped her legs around him, pulling him in even deeper.

"Oh, God, Grey." She felt the tide rise, flooding through her, washing her in bliss. "I'm coming."

As she began to wail in pleasure, she realized J.M. could probably hear her—damn, there was no way he couldn't hear her—yet the thought seemed to heat her blood all the more.

Was he getting turned on? Pleasure spiked through her and she wailed louder, imagining J.M. flinging open the door, then Grey lifting her up and J.M. sliding into her from behind. Her two men fucking her at the same time.

She moaned, then cried out as ecstasy erupted through every cell in her body.

Grey groaned and gushed inside her. He slowed his thrusts, kissing her cheek with loving tenderness.

J.M. heard Hanna's moans of pleasure from the bedroom.

His stomach muscles clenched. He pulled the blankets higher, tucking them around his ears, trying to block out the sound. He rolled over, facing the back of the couch, trying not to think of the fact that Grey was making love to Hanna in the next room.

"Oh, God, yes," her hoarse voice sounded through the wall.

J.M.'s fist clenched, even as his cock swelled to full erection. He was torn between flinging on his clothes and tearing out of the apartment and marching into that room and joining the two of them.

"Oh, God, Grey. I'm coming."

J.M.'s cock strained, demanding release, but he ignored it as his gut coiled tight, knowing she had just found ecstasy in Grey's arms.

Damn it, he'd been a total idiot coming here.

sixteen

Hanna woke up to warm sunshine on her face and the sound of Grey's slow, even breathing. In the warmth of Grey's embrace, she thought about J.M. in the next room. How he must have heard her and Grey making love last night. The thought turned her on immensely. In fact, even more, she was turned on by the fantasy that had flashed through her mind of J.M. rushing into the room and joining Grey in pleasuring her.

She sucked in a deep breath, unable to rid herself of the intense desire to experience both men at the same time. She had learned a lot about herself over the past few weeks. A deep sexual awakening had occurred within her.

If she wanted two men, why shouldn't she have two men?

She had done everything she could to assure Grey that she loved him. Last night, she had proven to him she could climax in his arms.

Now it was time to assure herself of some things. Like it was okay to go after what she wanted. To find the sexual satisfaction she desired so intensely.

She decided to take a risk.

Hanna pulled on her robe and headed toward the kitchen. J.M. stood by the sink drinking a glass of water.

"Oh. Hi," she said, her fingers curling around the front of her robe.

Her cheeks flushed at the thought of J.M. hearing her in the throes of passion, but at the same time her insides heated at the memory of how excited it had made her.

He looked fabulously sexy standing there in his charcoal tank top and briefs. She longed to run her fingers over the smooth fabric of his shirt, to feel his hard, muscular chest through the thin cloth, the tight definition of his muscles under her fingertips.

She blushed hotter at the thought that she'd just left Grey's arms and now she was getting turned on by the sight of J.M.

She remembered the pirate fantasy, when the two men had made love to her at once, and an incredible longing spiked through her.

Her gaze swung directly to J.M.'s. She knew what she wanted and she refused to be embarrassed by it. She loved Grey, but she wanted J.M., too. She had spent too many years allowing herself to shrink inside at the thought of how others might judge her. She had cared too much about what other people thought. What she had learned over the past few weeks was that what she wanted was important and the first step in getting what she wanted was allowing herself to know what that was. The second was going after it.

She wanted both Grey and J.M. . . . at the same time. And she planned to do something about it.

Her fingers relaxed, releasing the scrunched fabric of her robe, then she dragged her hand over her hip, then upward. J.M.'s gaze grew hot and hungry as it followed her hand.

He downed the rest of his water, then set the glass on the counter.

"I was just heading for the shower," he said.

He stepped past her, but she grasped his arm. He stopped, his gaze locking with hers. She moved toward him and slid her hand to his cheek. Saying nothing, she simply tipped up her head and leaned forward. He had to see the deep desire in her eyes. His mouth met hers with passion and power and she kissed him hungrily. His arms slid around her and pulled her tight against him, her breasts compressing against his hard, masculine chest.

"Ahem."

Hanna started at the sound of Grey clearing his throat behind her. She eased away from J.M. and dragged her gaze from his simmering chocolate eyes to Grey's glittering moss green ones.

The anger in Grey's eyes warred with the obvious hurt.

"Grey . . ."

"So you've decided you want him? You've had your orgasm with me, you're all healed, so now you can be with him. Is that it?"

She shook her head.

"Grey, it's not about that, it's—"

"I come out here and find you in his arms—kissing him—and right after we had the best sex ever." He slammed his fist on the counter. "What the hell am I supposed to think?"

"Grey, I've learned so much about myself over the past few weeks. You've helped me do that. The hypnosis, opening up my deepest, most hidden fantasies. You've helped me to see that I need to go after what I want. I need to allow myself to experience wild, sexy things if I want to. I need to realize that it's not wrong to do that."

She stepped toward him, wanting to reassure him, wanting him to understand. She grasped his cheeks in her hands.

"Grey, I love you." She leaned forward and pressed her lips to his. Sweet. Gentle. Showing him her love. "And I hope you'll help me on this journey of self-discovery. I have a feeling I have a lot of new and wonderful experiences ahead of me. I hope you'll be a part of them."

She kissed him again and this time he answered her kisses fiercely, his arms clamping around her, tugging her into his tight embrace. His tongue thrust into her mouth and she coiled hers around it. When he released her, she gasped for air.

She stepped backward and turned so she could see both men, then her finger tangled around the knot at her waist.

"J.M. . . ." She released the tie and allowed her robe to drop open.

Both men watched the fabric part, exposing a thin strip of shadowy, naked skin. She held her hand out to J.M. and he stepped forward, placing his hand in hers. She dropped the robe off her right shoulder and drew his hand to her breast. She glanced at Grey.

His fiery green eyes had darkened with heat. The feel of J.M.'s hand cupping her breast sent her head into a spin, but she held out her hand to Grey and he stepped forward. She dropped the robe to the floor, now totally naked before them. Grey cupped her other breast and she sighed at the exquisite pleasure of the two men she loved touching her in such an intimate way.

J.M. glanced toward Grey and said, "I am totally thrilled to be a part of this, but I need to know if you're okay with me being here."

In answer, Grey released her breast and stepped behind her. Then he slid his hands under Hanna's breasts and lifted them, as if offering them to J.M.

J.M. smiled and leaned forward to lick one hard nipple, then the other. Hanna dropped her head onto Grey's shoulder and moaned. J.M. settled on one nipple and drew it into his mouth. His tongue spiraled over the tip, then he sucked it into his hot, wet mouth. Grey gently twirled her other nipple between his fingertips.

Her blood heated to a slow boil. This was sheer heaven.

J.M. released her nipple to the cool air and Grey stroked the wet bud as J.M. captured her dry nipple in his mouth. He sucked it so deep and hard, she cried out.

Grey led her to one of the kitchen stools, easing her onto it, then drawing her back to rest against his chest. He tucked his hands under her knees and lifted her legs, opening them wide. J.M. accepted the invitation and settled on his knees in front of her, then began kissing her sensitive inner thighs. She moaned as his lips came close to the dripping wet flesh between her legs, then groaned as he veered away. Grey nuzzled her neck as he watched J.M. kiss up her thighs again.

This time J.M. dabbed his tongue against her clit and she cried out in pleasure. He spiraled over her tight nub, then danced over it in wild, gyrating swirls. She felt the pleasure rise and she arched up to meet him, but he backed away. The swell of pleasure dropped and she giggled, knowing she hadn't lost it. It would be all the stronger for his playing.

J.M. glanced at Grey and grinned, then grasped Hanna's legs and lifted them over his shoulders. As he stood up, her knees rose and her head sank until she hung upside down from his shoulders, his hands secure around her hips. Her hair hung straight up . . . er, down, from her head, and the delicious sensation of blood flowing to her head added to the feeling of light-headedness.

She watched Grey upside down as he dropped his robe, followed by his boxers. A moment later, he stood in front of her, his long cock jutting toward her. She grasped him and opened her mouth, sucking him like a lollipop. Hard and sweet. Filling her mouth with his hot, masculine flesh.

When she felt Grey's tongue push between her folds, she cried out. His cock fell from her mouth. He licked her once, then twice, then dove his tongue inside her.

"Oh, yes."

With a shaking hand, she grasped his cock again and brought it back to her mouth, concentrating on licking him as his mouth covered her. She drew him deep inside, swirling her tongue around his shaft, then twirled her lips around him as she drew him out again.

She licked and nibbled him as his tongue explored her slick opening. He dabbed at her clit, then sucked it, triggering a sudden swell of sensation.

"Oh, God, I'm going to come."

He sucked harder and she wailed.

"Right . . . ohhh . . . now."

She wailed, long and hard, as the orgasm crashed over her. Totally unexpected. Totally amazing.

As the pleasure subsided, she hung there, gasping for

air. She realized she was moving, and a moment later she felt herself being placed on the couch. She leaned against the back of the couch as each man leaned toward her and sucked a nipple into his mouth. She tucked an arm around each of them, loving the hot, hungry feel of man-mouth on her bare breasts. An incredible feeling of completeness filled her. Pleasure swelled and . . .

"Oh, my God," she gasped as another orgasm claimed her.

Going wild certainly had its rewards.

"My turn," she insisted as she grasped their hard cocks, one in each hand.

Somewhere along the way J.M. had shed his briefs and tank top.

She coaxed the two men to the couch as she stood up. She grasped them again as she knelt before the two of them, sitting side by side on the couch, their cocks at full attention.

She dabbed her tongue on the tip of J.M., then dipped her head and licked his cock from base to head. She switched to Grey and licked him the same way. When she returned to J.M. she wrapped her lips around him and swallowed his cock head into her mouth while swirling her hand around his shaft, then she dove deep, sucking him completely into her mouth and throat. She bobbed up and down, enjoying his groans of delight. She released him from her mouth, swirling her hand up and down his shaft as she sucked Grey deep inside, indulging him with the same treatment.

She shifted back and forth, sucking first one cock, then the other. She could tell Grey was very close, so she tucked her hand under his balls and dove down deep, then sucked hard, then pulsed up and down, up and down until he moaned. She squeezed him within her mouth and stroked his perineum and he stiffened and groaned, gushing into her mouth. She swallowed, then licked her lips.

She smiled and kissed him heartily. He slid his arms around her and kissed her soundly in response. Then she slid to J.M., kneeling in front of him.

She grinned at him.

"I know you pride yourself on keeping this thing erect . . ." She stroked his long, impossibly granite-hard cock. "But how about you humor me?"

He grinned back and bowed his head.

"Whatever your pleasure, my lady."

She licked his long shaft, then sucked him inside. As she did, Grey moved behind her, his hands caressing her buttocks in circles. J.M.'s gaze shifted from Hanna bobbing up and down on his cock to Grey stroking her ass. Grey's hand slid over her sensitive inner thighs, and she gasped as he dipped into her hot slit. J.M. twitched inside her mouth. She squeezed him, and Grey pushed two fingers, then three, inside her. His fingers moved in and out as she sucked on J.M. She knew she could have done a much better job pleasing J.M. if she hadn't been so distracted, but what she lost in technique seemed to be compensated for by his fascination at watching Grey toy with her. Pleasure swelled within her—and Grey pulled back. She concentrated on J.M., sucking and squeezing his deliciously hard cock, then started to ride a heady wave as Grey brought her close again.

"Ohhhh," she moaned around J.M.'s hard flesh, and she quivered, but Grey backed off again.

The third time he brought her close, she squeezed her mouth tightly around J.M. in reaction, then sucked hard. Grey backed off, but J.M. swelled and exploded in her mouth.

She concentrated on J.M., sucking his erupting cock as his whole body pulsed with pleasure.

When his cock stopped twitching, she released it, then licked her lips.

"You know, this woman has some pretty wild fantasies," Grey said to J.M.

"Really? I knew she had a wild side." He stroked his hand over her breast. "So what are these fantasies?"

When Grey didn't say anything, Hanna glanced toward him and realized he wouldn't reveal anything more if she didn't agree. She grinned and nodded, wanting to hear his take on it.

"She fantasizes about being ravaged by bikers." Grey curved his hand over her ass and squeezed. "Several of them—at the same time."

"Why, you naughty girl." J.M.'s grip on her breast tightened and her nipple hardened.

She eased herself up and grasped J.M.'s shoulders, then prowled over him, her knees on either side of his thighs. She wrapped one hand around his cock and stroked, but he was already rock hard and ready to go.

"Big, strong bikers in black leather." She smiled and stroked. "With big cocks." She shifted her pelvis over him. "Just like yours." She dropped down, impaling herself on his cock. The feel of it driving deep inside almost made her come right then, but she sucked in a breath and held it off.

She glanced over her shoulder at Grey and reached out her hand. He stepped forward and she grasped his cock, loving the feel of its familiar length in her hand. She stroked him.

"And yours."

She leaned forward, lifting her ass in the air. He stroked her round buttocks.

"The problem is, sweetheart, I don't have any lubricant."

"We could use her natural lubrication," J.M. suggested. He wrapped his hands around her hips and eased her upward, sliding out of her. She felt Grey nudge her vagina from behind, then slide his fingers into her. A second later, his big, hard cock slid inside her sex.

"Ohhhh."

He stroked several times, then slipped out. J.M. slid

back in and she groaned. Both men sliding their steel-hard cocks into her sent her hormones fluttering.

Grey's fingers toyed with her anus. First one masculine finger slipped inside, then another. They circled around, opening her. A third finger slid in and Grey gently coaxed her opening wider. J.M. stroked her breasts as his cock stood still inside her, stretching her with its mere presence.

Grey withdrew his fingers, then his cock head nudged at her opening. She tensed.

J.M. stroked her cheeks. "It's all right, honey. Just relax." He kissed her and she did relax. "When he pushes, you push, too," J.M. murmured. "That will open you so he can slide in."

On cue, Grey eased forward. Hanna pushed her muscles and Grey slid in. His cock head was buried inside her. She sighed.

J.M. kissed her mouth and Grey kissed the back of her neck while his hand slid around her and cupped her breast. J.M. cupped the other breast. She relaxed into their pleasure-giving attention.

Slowly, Grey eased farther in. His cock filled her, deeper and deeper.

J.M. filled her and so did Grey. She shifted a little and groaned at the intense pleasure.

J.M. began to move. Grey followed his rhythm. Both men gliding into her at the same time.

"Oh, yes." She clung to J.M.'s shoulders as the two

cocks thrust in and out, pulsing against each other inside her.

"Oh, my . . . this is . . . so . . ." Pleasure rocketed through her and she wailed.

"I'm coming. Oh, my God, I'm . . ."

She clung to J.M. and simply let them bounce her body between them as a lightning bolt of pure bliss ricocheted through every cell in her body, exploding in the wildest, most intense orgasm yet.

"That was incredible."

They carried her to bed and cuddled her between them.

She sighed and closed her eyes.

Sometime later, she woke up to both of them stroking her again.

"I could get used to this," she said as they both drew a nipple into their hot mouths.

J.M. slid his hot, hard cock into her and thrust gently until he brought her to a slow, languorous orgasm. She floated in a blissful heaven with his gentle strokes.

Grey entered her next and thrust a little harder and a little faster, bringing her to an intense climax, sending her senses rocketing to heaven.

"I love you," Grey murmured as they snuggled against her.

seventeen

Hanna woke up to find herself alone in the bed. She smiled as she remembered how exquisite this morning had been. The two men she loved bringing her to the heights of ecstasy. It was a fantasy come true.

She would have expected to feel embarrassment, and maybe some feelings of regret at acting so impulsively, but she didn't. She had wanted both men and she'd gone after them. She'd been wild and uninhibited and, as a result, all three of them had enjoyed a truly incredible, passionate experience.

She glanced around the room. Now where had they gone?

She pushed back the covers, then pulled on her robe. She opened the bedroom door and headed for the kitchen.

Grey sat at the table, drinking a cup of coffee and reading the paper. He was dressed in a business suit, ready for work.

blush

"Good morning." She grabbed a mug from the cupboard beside the stove, then ran her hand over Grey's shoulder as she sat down beside him, unable to resist touching him. "Where's J.M.?"

"Gone."

She frowned as she poured a cup of coffee from the stainless-steel carafe on the table. She hadn't thought about the fact that the two men might be uncomfortable with each other after what had happened earlier.

Had Grey said something to J.M.?

"Do you know why he left?" she asked.

"No, he was gone when I got up. His bag is gone, too. I assume he went back to Spring Falls."

Grey's tone seemed distant. She stared across the table at him . . . actually, at the back of his newspaper.

This wasn't like Grey. When they'd been together, he'd always put aside the newspaper whenever she'd come into the kitchen in the morning and they'd share a pleasant breakfast together. Yesterday had been the same.

She sat quietly, staring at the large pages facing her. The silence hung between them for several long moments.

Grey folded his paper and put it down, then took a sip of his coffee.

"I was thinking . . . ," he began.

He paused and her heartbeat seemed to flutter. She was certain she wasn't going to like where this was going.

Her fingers tightened around her hot mug as she lifted it to take a sip.

"It might be a good idea," he continued, "if you went back, too."

She stared at him, her cup halfway to her mouth. Slowly, she lowered the mug and placed it back on the table.

"You want me to leave?"

Her heart crumpled. He didn't want her here.

His lips compressed to a straight line.

"I just think it would be a good idea for both of us to have some space right now. To figure things out."

Had last night been too much for him? Sure, he'd gone along with it in the heat of the moment, caught up in the sexual excitement, but now . . . in the light of day . . . Had her wild side shocked him?

He stood up and walked across the room. The sound of the water running as he rinsed out his cup seemed to echo through the silence. He opened the dishwasher and placed the mug on the top rack, then closed the door.

"I'll call you in a few days," he said, then pushed open the kitchen door. A moment later, she heard the apartment door open and close.

He was gone.

She took a sip of her coffee, then pushed herself to her feet, feeling numb inside.

It was time to pack.

When Hanna got off the bus, Grace was there to meet her. Hanna had called her before she left New York, knowing she'd need the comfort of her big sister when she got home.

"Hanna." Grace threw her arms around Hanna and gave her a big hug. Hanna fought back the tears as her sister held her. "You okay, honey?"

Hanna nodded, even though she didn't feel at all okay.

On the drive home, she told Grace everything, from Grey catching J.M. and her together to J.M. showing up in New York to patch things up with Grey. The part where Hanna found out that J.M. was really Grace's friend Jeremy elicited a delighted response from Grace.

Hanna didn't tell Grace the wild details about that morning, but she did end with the fact that Grey had essentially thrown her out.

Grace parked in Hanna's driveway and followed her up the path to the entrance. Hanna unlocked the door, then put her suitcase in her bedroom. When she returned to the living room, Grace handed her a glass of lemonade and sat down beside her on the couch.

"Tell me exactly what happened. Did Jeremy and Grey fight over you?"

"Not exactly. I . . ."

Grace took her hand and gazed at her with somber

eyes. "Come on, honey. Whatever it is, you can tell me."

Hanna squeezed her hands into fists.

What would her sister think if she told her she'd taken part in a ménage à trois? Not just taken part. Instigated it.

Damn, she'd promised herself she wouldn't worry about what other people thought. Of course, that concept had totally blown up in her face!

Still, if she couldn't tell her sister, she hadn't made any progress at all.

"I . . . uh . . . suggested the three of us . . . Grey and J.M. and I . . ." Hanna hesitated.

"Yes?" Grace stared at her with avid curiosity.

Hanna cleared her throat, then decided to just go for it.

"I suggested a threesome."

Grace's face broke into a huge smile.

"Well, good for you, honey. Did they go for it?"

Hanna drew in a deep breath, both surprised and relieved at Grace's reaction.

Hanna nodded. Grace clapped her hands together and laughed.

"You lucky girl. Sandwiched between those two good-looking hunks."

"Except that J.M. was gone when I woke up, then Grey threw me out."

Grace rested her hand on Hanna's arm. "It sounds like Grey's having trouble dealing with it. He's the traditional type. He probably just needs time to adjust to the idea."

"Or maybe he won't adjust. Maybe he's decided he doesn't want someone like me in his life. Maybe . . ." A sob rose in her throat. "Maybe I've lost him for good."

Hanna turned into Grace's welcoming arms and let the tears fall.

Six excruciating, lonely days later, Hanna gathered her mail from the mailbox at her front door as she arrived home from work. A dark pink envelope caught her attention. It looked like a greeting card, but her birthday was still three months away and there were no other holidays coming up. Why would someone send her a card? And who?

Probably Grace.

Hanna dropped the other mail on the table and sat down, checking the back of the envelope for a return address. None. She flipped the envelope over and realized there was no stamp, either. It must have been hand delivered.

She pushed her fingernail under the flap of the envelope, tore it open, then pulled out the card.

On the front, she saw the words AN INVITATION in crimson script. She opened it.

Come to the Silver River Inn
9:00 this evening

That's all it said. No signature. Nothing to indicate whom it was from.

Could it be from Grey? Maybe he'd come to terms with her wild side and wanted her back? It could be from J.M. Maybe Grace had told him what happened and he wanted to start up their relationship again. On the other hand, it could be Grace trying to cheer her up—or send her on a blind date.

But it could be from Grey.

She glanced at her watch. Six thirty. She scurried to her feet and pulled together a quick dinner, then shot into the bathroom for a shower.

At 8:55, in makeup and her favorite little black dress, she climbed the stairs of the elegant stone building—one of the classiest hotels in town—the Silver River Inn.

Her heels clacked on the shiny marble floor as she walked across the lobby toward the concierge desk. Light glittered from a row of huge crystal chandeliers hanging from the ceiling, setting off the intricate carving on the arches above. Molded wood paneling adorned the walls along with several floor-to-ceiling pillars. Plush chairs in rose velvet, floral couches, and glass tables abounded, along with tall, green plants and huge flower arrangements in elegant ceramic pots.

"Ah, mademoiselle." A tall gentleman dressed in a sharp black suit approached her. "You are Miss Lane, correct?"

She nodded. He handed her a bouquet of long-stemmed dusky pink roses and a key.

"Your party awaits you in the Lavender Suite." He gestured to the right. "The elevators are there. Once you reach the seventh floor, simply turn right and go to the end of the hall. You will see it on your left."

"Thank you."

She sniffed the lovely fragrance of the roses as she rode the elevator up, then walked down the hall on rubbery legs. What would she find awaiting her in the Lavender Suite?

At the end of the hall, she stopped in front of the door, sucked in a deep breath, then knocked. When no one answered, she realized she held the key in her hand. An actual, physical key—old-fashioned and very elegant looking. She inserted it into the keyhole and turned, then pushed the door open.

A soft glow emanated from inside. As she stepped through the door, she realized there were candles all around the room, lighting it with a soft glow. What she saw was a lovely living area, with a couch and two chairs surrounding a round table. Beyond was a large window overlooking the river, which glittered in the light of the full moon.

She closed the door behind her and glanced around, anxious to see who had sent her the invitation. No one was in the room.

Several vases of flowers adorned the room and she noticed an empty vase filled with water on the round coffee table. She stepped toward the couch, peeled the clear cellophane off the bouquet of roses she held and placed the roses in the water, then sat down on the couch to wait for whatever would happen—almost afraid to hope that it was Grey who had invited her here.

"I've missed you."

Grey's voice. She turned to see him standing in a doorway behind her, looking stunningly handsome in a burgundy satin robe. The glowing light of the candles softly accentuated the planes of his exceptional body. Her heart soared with joy. She wanted him to sweep her into his arms, but he calmly crossed the room and sat down on one of the chairs facing her.

"I've missed you, too," said another male voice.

She glanced around and her breath caught as she noticed J.M. in the same doorway, looking just as handsome in an identical satin robe. He crossed the room and sat down on the other chair.

Oh, God, they were both here. Did they want to confront her about the other day? Or did they want a *repeat*?

"Hanna, I had some problems dealing with my feelings after the morning the three of us were together," Grey said.

So this was a confrontation.

She dropped her gaze to her hands folded in her lap. "I know."

"I . . . saw how much you enjoyed being with Jeremy and I didn't know how to deal with it."

Her gaze returned to Grey's face. She wanted to reach

out and hold him. To reassure him of how much she loved him.

Grey moved toward her, then knelt down and took her hand in his. His green eyes glittered in the candle-light, but it was the warmth of love in those depths that melted her heart.

"Hanna, I love you. I want you in my life always."

His soft breath brushed across the back of her hand as he kissed it, sending tingles through her.

"Will you marry me?"

Her breath caught. She glanced at J.M. and he smiled encouragingly.

If Grey was really proposing, why had he asked J.M. to be here?

"Sweetheart, I love you," Grey said, drawing her attention back to his glittering green eyes, full of hope and love. "I want us to spend a lifetime together."

"Yes." Her answer came out on a breath.

Grey swept her into his arms and kissed her. Then he released her and went back to his chair. To her total shock, J.M. stood up and stepped toward her, then knelt in front of her.

She watched, wide-eyed, as he took her hand. She glanced at Grey's smiling face and wondered what in hell they'd cooked up.

"Hanna, I love being with you." J.M. kissed the back of her hand, sending heat flooding through her. "Will you be my lover, with full approval and participation of your husband?"

Her wide-eyed gaze shifted from J.M. to Grey, then back again. Both men sported broad, encouraging smiles.

"Your . . . lover?" she practically squeaked.

She turned to Grey. "And you don't mind?"

"Sweetheart, you've discovered a wild, uninhibited side of yourself that I find intensely erotic. I want to encourage you." Grey grinned. "And I know I'll enjoy the benefits, too."

She turned back to J.M. "And why do you want to do this?"

He smiled and took her hand.

"I've found your sexual awakening to be very exciting and I'd like to continue to be a part of it. But more, I feel a strong connection with you. You bring a special light to my life." He stroked her cheek and the delicate touch of his fingertips sent tingles through her. "I see the love in your eyes when you're with Grey and I know the two of you are meant to be together, but I think I can have a place in your life, too. For as long as it feels right." He glanced at Grey. "For all of us."

Her blood heated and she squeezed J.M.'s hand.

"I'd have to be crazy to turn down a proposition like this." Her voice lowered. "And I'm not crazy."

J.M. smiled broadly. "So that's a yes?"

"Absolutely."

He cupped her cheeks and met her mouth with his.

His tongue gently stroked her lips, then delved inside. She opened to him, and sighed as the kiss turned passionate, letting her senses revel in the feel of his strong arms wrapping around her.

Then he released her.

Grey opened a cupboard on one wall and pulled out a flat box with a big red bow on top, then handed it to her. She fumbled with the ribbon, then pulled off the top. As she pushed aside the red tissue paper, she noticed black leather. She pulled out the garment. From the skimpy strips of leather hung silver chains. She wasn't quite sure how it worked, but it looked extremely sexy and her insides trembled.

Grey and J.M. both shed their robes, and they wore black leather pants. Grey had a leather vest with no shirt underneath and wore a thick chain around his neck. J.M. wore a black tank top, which showed off his bulging biceps, and he pulled on black fingerless gloves with silver studs.

"Why don't you go put it on?" J.M. asked, gesturing toward the little leather whatsit they'd given her. "The bathroom's that way." He pointed toward a door off to the left, then handed her a shoe box. "Take these, too."

She slipped into the large bathroom and switched on the light. A large mirror reflected back her pink-tinged face. Excitement. Not embarrassment.

Quickly, she shed her clothing, then pulled on the tiny garment. She stepped into what seemed to be the leg openings of the thong portion and slid it up over her hips. She stared down at it, trying to figure how to put on the top, and realized the bra portion consisted of straps surrounding the breasts in a triangle shape and chains draping over each breast. She pulled it on, exhilarated by the feel of the cold, silver chains brushing against her nipples. Five chains over each breast and . . . oh . . . each center chain had a metal ring in the middle that sat right over her nipple.

As she adjusted the leather straps so it sat just right, her nipples blossomed, sticking forward through the rings.

She opened the shoe box to find a pair of black leather shoes with four-inch spike heels and ankle straps with silver studs. She pulled the shoes on and fastened the straps, then glanced at herself in the mirror. Her eyes widened. She looked . . . erotic . . . wicked . . . and wildly sexy.

She noticed a chain draped over the crotch of her leather outfit. She flicked it with her finger and realized there was a slit in the fabric beneath it, running the length of the crotch. *Oh, heavens.*

She opened the door and stepped into the living room. Both men rose to their feet, their gazes riveted on her.

Her hand strayed to her breast and she stroked the chains back and forth over her rigid nipple. J.M. stepped toward her, Grey right behind him. J.M. stroked the chain aside with his fingertips, then covered her nipple with his mouth. Grey leaned straight to her breast and stroked his tongue around the inside of the ring encircling her nipple, driving her wild, then lapped at the tip.

She moaned. Dampness pooled in her vagina and she feared it would drip through the slit in her crotch and down her thighs.

She curled her arms around their heads and led them toward the couch, where she eased herself down, clinging to them still.

"Are you two bikers going to ravage me?"

"Absolutely," Grey answered.

They each took one of her arms and eased her to her feet, then practically lifted her from the floor as they swept her into the bedroom. She felt them wrap something around her wrists and realized it was leather straps with rings attached. They laid her on the bed and stretched her arms wide, then fastened her wrists to the headboard.

Then they grabbed her ankles and attached straps, then fastened her spread-eagled to the footboard.

Grey sat on the side of the bed and toyed with one of the chains on her chest, rolling it over her tender, throbbing nipple. J.M. sat at the end of the bed and pushed the chain on her crotch until it rubbed the sensitive flesh between her legs. He pressed it against her clit, back and forth. The cold metal rolling over her sensitive nub sent intense sensations throbbing through her.

"She's so wet," J.M. told Grey.

"Let me see." Grey moved to the end of the bed and slid his finger along her slit.

He leaned forward and licked her, then dabbed at her

clit. J.M. unfastened his leather pants and drew out his erection. As he stepped to the side of the bed, she turned her head and opened her mouth. He fed it to her and she sucked and licked as he glided forward and back.

Grey continued to lick her clit and she arched against him.

"She is so ready," Grey said. He prowled onto the bed. His cock pressed against her and then . . .

She moaned around J.M.'s cock as Grey thrust himself into her wet opening. Hanna sucked J.M. greedily as Grey thrust into her. Soon pleasure careened through her. Grey drove into her, hard and fast, then groaned as he climaxed. J.M. pulled free of her mouth, as Grey climbed off her. J.M. moved over her, then drove his cock into her. Long. Hard. Thrusting deep and fast.

"Yes. . . ." She moaned. "God, that's . . . oh . . . so good."

She felt a climax approach and she welcomed it. It swept over her and, as she wailed, J.M. shot his seed deep into her.

J.M. eased from her body, then sat on the end of the bed again. Grey sat beside him. The two of them stroked her inner thighs, from knee to her sex and then back again. Teasing. Stroking. Although she'd come to orgasm once, she knew they weren't finished with her yet. J.M. leaned forward and licked her slit. Grey's fingers stroked over her clit. J.M. jabbed his tongue inside her, then slid two fingers into her. He stroked her inner walls until an intense pleasure began to build.

Oh, God, he knew where the G-spot was. Well, of course he knew. If anyone did, it would be him. As he stroked, she felt a wild, compelling hunger build within her, then a mind-blowing pleasure sweep through her. The orgasm exploded in a liquid gush.

She slumped on the bed. Her whole body felt aglow.

Grey and J.M. unfastened her wrists and ankles, then Grey sat on the edge of the bed and drew her onto his lap. She wrapped her legs around him as he stroked her back lovingly. As he slid his hands to her hips, J.M. stood behind her and slid his hands over her breasts. Her nipples—hard, tight, and sensitive—peaked into his palms. Grey caressed her hip, then slid one hand down her belly to her damp folds. As he stroked her clit, intense sensations exploded through her. She moaned and J.M. cupped her breasts more firmly. His lips caressed the back of her neck and tingles raced along her spine. Grey's hard cock glided inside her. His hands slid to her behind and he grasped her firmly, holding her tight against him, his cock deep inside her. He lifted her and she felt J.M.'s swollen cock head nudge against her back opening. It felt slippery and warm. He pushed forward, sliding into her, stretching her in a lovely, erotic invasion.

Grey began to move and J.M. matched the slow, rhythmic thrusting.

She clung to Grey as the two of them thrust into her, filling her with their rock-hard maleness, stretching her passages. She felt so cherished . . . with both men holding her . . . making love to her. Exquisite pleasure built within her. Higher and higher.

Their cocks seemed to expand as they stroked her insides, sending her to a state of bliss. She gasped, then moaned as their semen exploded into her, triggering her own cataclysmic orgasm. She wailed at the incredible, mind-blowing ecstasy careening through her body. Stunning in its intensity.

She clung to Grey as she relaxed within the heat of their hard, muscular bodies. This was how it would be. Every day if she wanted. For as long as she wanted.

And who knew what other adventures might come her way, especially with two such understanding men, who clearly didn't mind sharing.

epilogue

Hanna yawned as she shuffled to the front door, her fingers feebly attempting to tie her robe around her waist. The doorbell rang again.

It had been four days since her proposals and she'd gotten very little sleep, surprising considering how much time she'd spent in bed.

She pulled open the door to see Grace staring at her.

The minute Grace saw Hanna in her robe, she knew there'd be no running today.

"Don't tell me you forgot again. You were the one who suggested doing this running thing, you know?"

"I know. I've been a bit distracted lately."

Grace stepped past her yawning sister and closed the door behind her. She dropped her bag and running shoes by the door, then kicked off her sandals. The delicious aroma of gourmet coffee wafted in the air.

"I need caffeine." Grace headed for the kitchen.

"Grey bought an automatic coffeemaker," Hanna said as she followed Grace across the living room.

Grace stopped in her tracks. "Grey? Are you two back together again?"

"You bet." Grey stepped through the kitchen door with a tray containing four mugs of coffee, cream, sugar, and spoons and placed it on the coffee table.

"In fact, we're engaged." Hanna held up her hand and wiggled her fingers. The sunlight from the window glistened off a lovely marquise diamond in a white gold setting.

"Oh, my gosh, that's wonderful." Grace flung her arms around her sister and hugged her tightly. "I'm so happy for you."

She was a little sad J.M. had lost out, but now that Grey had learned to express his feelings, she knew he would make her Hanna very happy.

"When did this all happen?"

"A few days ago. Sorry I didn't call you, but . . ." Hanna glanced at Grey with a twinkle in her eye. "We've been busy."

Grace pursed her lips in mock disapproval.

"Okay, I'll forgive you this time."

She sat down beside Hanna and grabbed a cup from the tray, then added sugar and cream to her coffee.

As Grace took a sip, she glanced at the tray. Grey had taken a cup and Hanna reached for hers.

One mug still sat on the tray.

"So why the fourth mug?" she asked.

Hanna glanced at Grey, a small smile turning up her lips.

J.M. stepped out of the bedroom, a towel loosely draped around his hips, and walked across the room. He leaned over and kissed Hanna on the cheek.

"Good morning, sweetheart." He sat down on the easy chair across from them, then helped himself to the fourth mug. "Morning, Grace."

Grace's gaze shifted from Grey in his T-shirt and boxers, to J.M. wrapped in a towel, his hair still damp from his shower, to Hanna in her robe.

"What in heaven's name is going on?"

Hanna put down her cup and smiled at Grace. "Well, I'm marrying Grey, but . . . J.M. is going to . . . uh . . . be part of the relationship."

"The three of you? Together?"

Hanna searched her face, clearly seeking approval, but Grace knew darned well she would go ahead with this arrangement whether she got it or not. Grace stared from one serious face to the next, then broke out laughing. She took Hanna's hand and squeezed gently.

"Honey, from now on, as far as love is concerned, I'm coming to you for advice."

acknowledgments

First, I thank my husband, Mark, and my sons for their support and love, and for their understanding during the days I've been cranky and sleep deprived because I extended myself a little too much. Mark is my greatest fan. He accompanies me to conferences, trade shows, and book signings. He gushes to "the ladies on the bus" about my books. He helps with all kinds of details, big and small, that would otherwise take me away from writing. There are no words to express how important he is to me, or how much I love him.

As always, I would like to thank Colette for her help in reading and commenting on my work, for the great suggestions she makes, and for the wonderful encouragement she offers.

I would like to thank LeeAnn for her help, not during the writing process, but in keeping me organized and motivated at book signings, spreading the word about my books, and generally encouraging me in all kinds of ways.

acknowledgments

Thanks to Rose Hilliard, my wonderful editor, for treating my books with tender, loving care and for being patient and supportive. Thanks to Emily for going above and beyond the call of duty as an agent. You are both gems and I'm glad we're a team.

Next, I would like to thank Melissa Lavender, a lovely young woman who works at Outback Steakhouse. Something she said—actually, delicately asking if I wrote books that "might make her blush"—gave me the idea for the title of this book. When I ran it by the powers that be at St. Martin's, they loved it.

I would like to acknowledge Pala Copeland and Al Link, who have been practicing Tantra since 1987 and work as Tantric sex teachers and relationship coaches. They offer Tantra and relationship weekend retreats for couples, which I highly recommend. My husband and I attended one of Pala and Al's retreats several years ago and I referenced the material from their workshop and several of their books in writing *Blush*. That provided me with wonderful details to work into the story. (Any errors are mine.) I recommend their books *The Complete Idiot's Guide to Supercharged Kama Sutra* and *Sensual Love Secrets for Couples,* as well as the other wonderful books they've published. Check their Web site for more information about their books and workshops at www.tantra-sex.com.

I would also like to acknowledge a great book I found while researching hypnosis called *Look into My Eyes: How*

acknowledgments

to Use Hypnosis to Bring Out the Best in Your Sex Life by Peter Masters. I used the induction scripts from his book as a guide for the hypnosis sessions in *Blush*. (Again, any errors are my own.)

Read on for a preview of Opal Carew's
upcoming erotic romance
Six,
available from St. Martin's Griffin in January 2009.

Harmony and her old college friends are respectable, straitlaced professionals, but once a year they reunite at an exotic resort for a decadent sexual free-for-all, complete with group sex and tantalizing erotic games. This year, Cole is finally going to reveal his true feelings for his old friend Harmony. But when she shows up with a new boyfriend in tow, she finds herself torn between two very stimulating men. . . .

Harmony stared at the glossy pamphlet again, with the photos of vivid blue tropical water, white sandy beaches, lovely villas along the water . . . and frowned. Aiden would be here in a few minutes.

Was she going to tell him her secret, or would she continue to keep it from him—just like she had with everyone else over the past twelve years?

Her heart clenched. For the first time in her life, she felt she had met a man she might have a future with—and she didn't want to endanger that.

But the time had come to make a decision.

Would she tell him? Or wouldn't she?

At the rat-a-tat-tat of small pellets hitting her apartment window, she glanced at the view beyond the glass.

Not that there was anything to see but swirls of snow. The eerie sound of the cold winter wind sent shivers through her. She glanced at the pamphlet again, laid out on her dark-stained cherry desk in her living room. Stroking her finger along the palm trees bathed in golden sunlight, she imagined the sun warming her bikini-clad body and fine sand pushing between her toes as she walked barefoot along the beach. The rhythmic sound of the surf washing along the shore drew her further into the lovely world of tropical heat and no worries as she left the cold, wintry world of Buffalo, New York, behind her.

The doorbell rang and Harmony folded up the pamphlet and stuck it in her desk drawer.

She crossed to the fireplace and flicked the switch to start the fire—she loved having a gas fireplace—then she answered the door.

"Hi, sweetheart." Aiden's cinnamon brown eyes glowed with warmth as he smiled at her, revealing a charming dimple in his cheek and softening the line of his strong, square jaw. She wanted to run her fingers through the dark brown waves of his wind-tousled hair, still aglitter with big, fat snowflakes.

He stomped his boots to knock off the snow still clinging to them even after his walk to the elevator, then down her hallway. He handed her his burgundy jacket, still covered with a sprinkling of soft, powdery snow, and she hung the coat in the closet as he kicked off his boots and stood them on the dark-green-and-brown woven mat by the door.

"Come here." He grinned as he grabbed her and pulled her into his arms.

His nose and cheeks were red and his skin was cold to the touch as his lips met hers hungrily. His arms came around her and her nipples hardened when his cold body pressed against her warm one, but as their kiss heated, she forgot all about the cold.

Finally, their lips parted and his gaze met hers.

"I've missed you," he said.

She smiled and drew back, taking his hand and leading him into the living room.

"It's only been two days."

His arm hooked around her waist and he nuzzled her ear.

"Two days too long, as far as I'm concerned."

They sat on the couch in front of the fireplace and snuggled together.

"Hot chocolate?" she asked.

He nodded and she poured them both a mug from the stainless steel carafe sitting on the tray on the coffee table in front of them. She knew how he loved hot chocolate, so she'd prepared a batch before he arrived, sure that he'd appreciate a cup to help him warm up after his drive here through the blizzard.

She really enjoyed Aiden's company and they had a lot in common. She had met him almost a year ago on a local ski trip to Kissing Bridge ski area in Glenwood—actually two weeks after she'd returned from her annual "vacation."

Leena, one of her friends from work, had talked her into going and, a total novice, Harmony had gone down the hill too fast and fallen, her legs twisted and her skis crossed in an awkward jumble.

Aiden had whooshed to a stop in an impressive spray of powder and helped her to her feet, no small task given that her skis kept sliding out from under her. Somehow he'd managed to get her vertical again and safely down the hill. He'd spent the afternoon coaching her and soon had her going down the hill in a somewhat competent manner, if not with grace and speed.

Now they'd been together for almost a year, and she couldn't go away on vacation without telling him about—

"You seem deep in thought. Anything you want to share?"

"No, I . . . uh, was just thinking about work and . . . I'm going to be taking a week off soon—to go on vacation."

"Oh?" He tightened his arm around her shoulders, drawing her closer to the warmth of his body. "Do you want to go somewhere together?"

"Actually, I've already made plans with friends."

"Really?" His eyebrows arched. "You haven't mentioned anything about it."

"I know. I've been meaning to tell you about it. . . ."